WHEN THE CUCKOO CALLS

The past is not as it appears

By

Michael Skelding

MAPLE
PUBLISHERS

When the Cuckoo Calls

Author: Michael Skelding

ISBN 978-1-83538-680-4 (Paperback)
   978-1-83538-681-1 (E-Book)

Cover Design nd Book Layout by:
   White Magic Studios
   www.whitemagicstudios.co.uk

Published by:
   Maple Publishers
   Fairbourne Drive, Atterbury,
   Milton Keynes,
   MK10 9RG, UK
   www.maplepublishers.com

A CIP catalogue record for this title is available from the British Library.

This Book is Dedicated to
Noel Hollingsworth
and
Norman Wooldridge

CONTENTS

Chapter One

Stepping Street

The little terraced houses followed the extreme steepness of the street and dropped down in tiered fashion. A March morning sun came up at right angles to the street and peered over the tops of the houses throwing shafts of sunlight to the one side leaving the other in shadow. The houses, once identical in every detail, now reflected various tastes of individual owners. Uniformity giving way, to the needs of modernisation and the desires of people to be different. One house, however, still retained its sash windows and the ornate terracotta lintels above each window. Its smooth red tight jointed brickwork had neither been cladded or rendered over and painted as was becoming the fashion. The original six panelled front door with its stained-glass half-moon fanlight above it still allowed the beams to enter at odd angles, as it did on this crisp morning to highlight her lifelessness as she sat positioned in a brocade winged armchair with her head back and slightly to one side.

Positioned and surrounded by a lifetime's collection of porcelain figurines thoughtfully placed on pretty lace doilies along with family photographs in gilt frames all sitting on a walnut sideboard and matching occasional tables. Surrounded by carefully chosen etchings and paintings and framed ancient maps hung in such a way that they all complimented each other. On the black marble mantlepiece above the Victorian fireplace with its William de Morgan tiles either side of the opening sat a drum head marble clock ticking away to matching black marble owls sitting each side of the clock, and above the fireplace hung a beautifully painted Campanula housed in a delicately carved ebony frame.

The geniality of Albert Hackett, or Bert, as he was affectionately known, knew no bounds. Even in those still dark unearthly hours when he delivered his daily pints to awaiting doorsteps exchanging empties for silver, or blue, or gold tops, his contentment was obvious. The odd insomniac would lie awake listening to the stopping and starting of his electric milk float and the clinking of bottles and his whistling rendition of some pre-rock sentimental ballad as he crisscrossed the street at a speed that belied his age. He was a man who was plainly happy in his own skin but was not so cheerful when noting that Mrs Campbell's doorstep was empty of empties for two days running and being now a worried man decided to investigate. He rang the doorbell and waited but no one came. He lifted the flap of the letter box and shouted her name but received no reply. If she had left for a holiday, she would have told him but she had not. So, he lifted the flap again to look in and the light from the street lamp just about allowed him to see her. Anyone else might have thought she was asleep but his wartime experiences made him instantly suspicious and he raced to the call box at the bottom of the street to dial 999.

Samuel Salt stood in his new office looking down on the town of his birth and his upbringing. His return after his time in the forces followed by his years at Scotland Yard had not been intended, yet here he was again seeing his best laid plans being overruled by the fateful forces that seemed to steer him. Even when determined to turn to the right the brick walls appeared and he was steered to the left, but he eventually learned not to regret the roads not taken by realising that he was where he was meant to be. It had happened throughout his life and was happening now, even though the thought of returning had never even entered his head until he was approached. But Samuel Salt was not a happy man. The town that he had come back to bore no resemblance to the town he had left all those years ago and what he found saddened him.

From his standpoint he could look across to The Scala where the Saturday morning kids club always started with a singalong before the cartoons brought exaggerated laughter from the boys and giggles from the girls. It was the only cinema left from the four that were there up until he left. One was now empty and derelict, the second a lap dancing club and the third a cut price supermarket.

He recalled being thrilled by the likes of Gene Autrey or Roy Rogers or Hopalong Cassidy on Topper riding the prairies fighting the Indians or the baddies. Flash Gordon would whisk him and his mates off into space before ending up in some dire predicament you knew he could not escape from until the following week. The National Anthem brought moans and vows from the boys never to stand again, but they always did. They also quickly became young men sitting in the same seats with their arms around a new sweetheart catching glimpses of the latest film between kisses. He remembered taking her there for the first time and afterwards walking hand in hand along the High Street looking into the well-lit shutterless shop windows admiring suits and dresses and jewellery, and a few years later picking out furniture for their future home when they eventually married.

He remembered the tobacconists with its wonderful displays of pipes and engraved silver cigarette cases and lighters and the exotic brands of cigarettes he would buy along with a determination not to live in the Woodbine world of his father. To enter was to walk into a treasure trove of aromas that seemed to emanate from the dozens of cigars on show. Many of them housed in boxes that were themselves little works of art. It came to mind how she once pointed out a pretty powder compact, only to find it a few weeks later as a surprise Christmas present. He recalled the exact spot where they first met and strolling home alone beneath a star-studded moonlit sky after a long and lingering goodnight kiss thinking that the world was his oyster and singing. That'll be the day.

Along with another way of life, most of those shops had now gone. The tobacconists had gone. Millets and Mace along with its wood panelled Dickensian aura and packed bookshelves and its unenforced library hush which had served generations no longer lured its customers to select some favourite author and take the book to a comfortable red leather brass studded armchair. Nowhere now for a sixteen-year-old to pick up a special offer from the bargain table and open it and stand transfixed by lines that would send shivers down his spine and affect his life for ever. No Hepworth's or Burtons to offer a young man the choice of being measured for his first bespoke suit and give him that feeling of proudly walking out after the final fitting and feeling like a million dollars. There were even rumours that The Scala was facing closure. The cinema where his grandmother in her late teens thoroughly enjoyed ushering excited customers to their seats for the latest silent film until her life was blighted by the already married pianist getting her pregnant. Secrets and lies eventually revealed by his mother who always carried the stigma of being illegitimate and desperately wanted to know who her real father was but was told to let sleeping dogs lie.

He pictured himself and Pete and Stinky in The Galleon making one cup of coffee last all evening while Be Bop a Lula and Three Steps to Heaven played over and over on the juke box. Pete who had taught him to play chess and who died too early but was missed more than he would ever know. Never to be forgotten times. Magical times. Young times interrupted by National Service. One in the army, one in the navy, and the other in the air force. Musketeers with their vows of always remaining mates butchered by the ways of the world. He wondered what the teenagers of today with their modern exotic coffee houses would make of The Galleon and its corny nautical interior. Another world, he thought. Another me, he thought. The times, as a rasping voice kept reminding them, were most certainly changing.

It was Benson who broke his chain of thought by lightly tapping on the door and then entering. "Morning Benson," said Salt while offering his sergeant a smile.

"Morning sir," said Benson, and then informed his boss that there had been a report of a possible murder.

"Local?" asked Salt.

"Yes sir."

"Whereabouts?"

"A terraced house in Stepping Street."

"And who reported this possible killing?"

"The local milkman," replied Benson.

"And would that milkman be Albert Hackett?"

"Yes sir, do you know him?"

"Only through him delivering to my parents up at The Spinney, but I thought he would be well retired by now."

"Apparently she had not left empties out for two days and that worried him so he peered through the letterbox and saw her dead in her chair."

"Perhaps she had died in her sleep."

"That is what he thought at first but the positioning of her head made him suspicious."

"I know he is ex-army," said Salt, "so he would have seen things."

"He seemed pretty confident," said Benson.

"Did she live alone?"

"Yes sir, according to Hackett she was a widow."

"And the name of his customer?" asked his boss.

"It's a Mrs Penelope Campbell," replied Benson while referring to his notebook.

"Lizzie White's sister," whispered Salt, almost to himself.

"You knew her," asked Benson.

"Many years ago," Salt replied with a faraway look, "They briefly came into my life" After giving Benson his orders regarding visiting the house and arranging for the team to meet in The Blue Room in the afternoon he asked for a few minutes to himself and turned once more to look out across the town. To look across to the sixteenth century turrets of the school he should have attended and beyond the school to the extra thin spire of St Cuthberts. One constant he thought in these ever-changing times, that had been around since first serving a tiny hamlet some seven hundred years ago and now served a conurbation that those early parishioners could not have even dreamt of. And what of the next seven hundred years, he contemplated, while taking his ever-present touchstone from his trouser pocket and rolling it round in the palm of his hand as a large black ominous cloud formed over the turrets and the spire. Will there even be a church or parishioners, he asked himself as the phone started ringing.

"It's only me," she said, "just checking you will be back for dinner."

"I think we have a killing Mary," he said.

"And that means?" she asked, but knew full well what it meant.

"That means it's doubtful," he replied.

"That means no," she said.

"Probably," he answered.

"You hinted that would not happen once back here," she replied in a rather annoyed tone.

"But it's a killing Mary," he said, "and you well know how much there is for me to organise."

"And you well know you could get someone else to cover for a couple of hours this evening," she said, while trying to keep the sarcasm to a minimum.

"Now look Mary," he said.

"No, you look Sam, I have sat home alone too many times and I have cancelled too many arrangements too many times and I have served up too many reheated dinners too many times and we are getting older all the time and I am thinking it is about time you finished. It was bad enough in London but at least I had my connections. You do have your work here Sam but I have nothing. We have returned to a town that we no longer know and no longer knows us."

At that she slammed the phone down but kept her hand on the receiver as the guilt engulfed her over the outburst. No one knew more than her about the almost spiritual dedication he gave to his work. He stood with the phone in his hand for a long time before sitting and carefully placing it back onto its cradle. His eyes were drawn to the black and white photo of them on his desk taken at the local ballroom just after his demob and their move to London. The guilt rose in him too, but surely the alignment was as true and strong for this as when they were brought together all those years ago. How could it be ignored? Things would be OK. He was sure. Maybe children would have made a difference but…

Benson entered this time without knocking to tell his boss that all arrangements had been made. Salt thanked him and then asked what he would do if he retired. His sergeant was taken aback by the question but eventually answered. "I think, I would retire also sir."

"But you're a good copper," said Salt, "at your age it would be a waste. You could easily follow on from me."

"Thank you for saying so sir," said Benson, "but I don't have what you have and without it I would always feel under-armed."

"And what is that I have?" asked Salt"

"That rests with you telling me." Answered his sergeant.

Now it was Salts turn to be taken aback by this shaft of wisdom coming from a man he had probably taken for granted for far too long. A man he had never shared his reasoning with although he always expected him to share his, but how do you explain that which is not always explainable, even to yourself?

After being left alone he returned once more to the window to look out on the turrets and the spire now being backed by the bluest of cerulean skies. A blueness that brought to mind a questioning phrase he had only read days before.

Where do all the clouds go?

Chapter Two

The Cuckoo's Call

Lizzie White was forever falling in and out of love. Not even marriage prevented her desired dalliances. And with a husband who was prepared to turn a blind eye there were many. Fidelity never figured in a union that allowed each other to plough their own furrows. He was thirty years her senior and had never expected such youthful vivacity to come into his life. For vivacious she most certainly was, with a confident beauteousness that lit every room she entered and she knew it. He was as astonished at her acceptance of his proposal after just a few dates as she was at finding such a man so early who would deliver in the way she believed she was entitled to. The move to the house on the hill with its many rooms and gated driveway was an expectation realised. Providence had provided as she always knew it would. The affairs were mostly short with disposed suitors soon forgotten. The remembered ones were the ones who spurned her flirting advances like the handsome young P.C. sent to investigate a burglary. He had never left her mind and she had followed his career and was aware of him coming back to the town and wondered if he would come to see her about the death of her sister. She still remembered him not accepting the offered glass of sherry and more, along with the polite smile that came with the refusal and how it accentuated a handsomeness that lived with her still.

"You don't know what you're missing," she had said.

"I have everything I need," he had replied, and walked away.

A bold statement she thought from someone so young and wondered if his future years would prove him wrong.

The desecration of Stepping Street displeased him deeply. It was a street he had always liked, even as a naïve ragged arsed council house kid delivering its daily papers. He did not know why he liked it but he did. It differed from all the other terraced houses in the town by having such intricate details carried through on each one. He recollected walking its length with not a car in sight telling Colly, and Colly, who delivered the odd numbers while he delivered the evens on the opposite side, replied with raised eyebrows and a shrug of the shoulders.

"It's just a bloody street Salty," he had said, "it's just a bloody street."

But it was more than just a street to Salt and he reckoned that if Colly had bought one of its houses over the years it would surely be the one with the lookalike stone cladding covering original exquisite brickwork.

"And you are just a bloody philistine," he had said to his friend who was opening a packet of Players stolen from over the counter that morning. It was a crime the young Salt wanted no part of, so when Colly offered him one he made the excuse of not liking Players and reached for his pack of Park Drive bought with his paper round money.

"Oh yeah and what's a bloody philistine then," asked Colly as they puffed their way down the street feeling much older than their years.

"A philistine," said his friend in his best head master's voice, "is someone who cannot appreciate that for over one hundred years all kinds of people have lived in this street experiencing the choreography of life."

"And what the bloody hell's that supposed to mean?" said Colly.

"It' means exactly what it says," said the young Salt, feeling quite superior while repeating a line he had only recently read and loved the sound of, and Colly, who thought of his mate as a right clever bastard, made the decision not to question him and appear ignorant.

Benson was getting edgy sitting in the Rover opposite the house of the victim but sensed his boss was on some kind of nostalgia trip. He could also see that the uniformed constable guarding the front door was wondering why they had not made a move. But Salt was giving the scene the "extra eye" as he called it. The eye that allowed access to that which can be so easily overlooked. The eye that also pictured himself knocking on that very door to collect the weekly paper money and it being opened by a captivating young lady with a smile that warmed his insides but he did not know why. He remembered Colly saying, "She bloody fancies you Salty," and him telling Colly not to be so bloody daft even though through his naivety he was not quite sure what being fancied meant but Colly seemed to know all about such stuff.

They approached the constable with their warrant cards and he offered to open the front door for them but Salt said he would prefer to use the entry and enter the house from the rear. The left-hand door at the end of the entry opened on to a terracotta paved courtyard with several plant pots holding a variety of evergreens and a rustic bench that when sat upon would allow observance of the long garden and the distant One-Way Wood.

At the back of the bench was the door that led immediately into the kitchen which was an extension to the original building. Salt could still picture the blue brick courtyards and the coalhouse and the outside toilets that accompanied every dwelling. Courtyards that now housed those kitchen and bathroom extensions. He even remembered the black faced coalmen humping their sacks before dumping their contents into the coalhouse.

On entering the kitchen, they were surprised to find thirties styled green and cream units with Formica worktops and a free-standing cooker and a Belfast sink and a tall dresser that matched the units. All sitting on a look alike linoleum floor. In the middle of the kitchen sat a small upcycled table and two chairs.

"I like it," said Benson.

"So do I," said Salt.

"Vintage but very new," observed Benson.

"It is almost a work of art," said Salt.

"Reminds me of my grandmother's kitchen," said Benson.

A glass panelled door led to a sitting room that contained an upright piano, a sideboard, a writing bureau and two leather rockers. The two chairs were placed facing a tiled fireplace which had a brass coal scuttle and companion set to match sitting on its hearth. There was no television, but on a small cabinet left of the fireplace sat a Bakelite wireless which reminded Salt of the nights he would stay up with his mother listening to Dick Barton or Journey into Space or P.C. 49, while his father was out drinking with his mates. It was the latter programme that first gave him the idea of becoming a copper.

"My mother used to swoon over Bing Crosby on one of these," he told Benson, while running the palm of his hand across the Bakelite to rekindle yet another memory. If Benson had heard him, he did not reply. He was studying the framed pencil drawings on the art deco papered walls, every one signed *P C Campbell*.

"Now this lady was seriously gifted," he almost mumbled to himself.

"And not just for drawing," said Salt.

"You mean the house as well," said Benson, picking up his boss's thinking.

"Absolutely," came the reply, "it's a work of art in itself."

"Did you actually know her sir?" asked Benson.

"I used to deliver newspapers in this street when I was a thirteen-year-old kid with my mate Colly," answered Salt. "And met her on a couple of occasions when collecting the money on Sundays but mostly it was her husband who paid."

"Then in my early twenties," he continued, "as a rookie copper before doing my stint in the army and then moving on to London I had to go up to Moss House to gather information about a burglary from a Mrs White. Now Mrs White so reminded me of Mrs Campbell that I asked her if she had a sister and she smiled and questioned me about meeting her twin."

Salt then turned towards the door that would allow them into the front room. They both entered with a reverence that needed no words and stood looking down at the body. Even when they did speak it was in hushed tones.

"I think that Hackett was right," whispered Salt.

"You think so," said Benson.

"I am convinced," said his boss.

"Even like this she does not look her age," said Benson.

"When they were young, they were both quite beautiful," said Salt, and pointed to the couples wedding photograph on an occasional table beside her chair. Next to it was a sepia photograph of the twins aged about twenty, both dressed in khaki standing next to nineteen forties army issued motor cycles.

"I see what you mean," whispered Benson.

"Must have done their bit in the war," said Salt.

"Beautiful indeed," said Benson as he picked up the photographs with his handkerchief for a closer look.

Although he wanted to close her eyes Salt knew he should not, but while they were open, he could not help but be drawn to them, and being drawn to them disturbed him deeply. They may have been lifeless but they seemed to look right through him as the eyes of the dead often do. It was a questioning stare that brought no answers.

"Perhaps you will go and find something to cover her," he whispered to Benson.

"Will do," said his sergeant and quietly left the room.

His boss tried to picture those kind eyes looking down on him as he stood on the doorstep and she stood framed in the doorway. Kind eyes that would never again warm the heart of a naïve innocent adolescent.

Benson returned with a sheet from an upstairs bedroom and after he had carefully placed it over her turned his attention to the etchings and the ancient maps and paintings while noting that none of them this time carried her signature.

"I like the purple bellflower," said Salt, pointing to the Campanula over the fireplace.

"She had wonderful taste," said Benson.

"Have you thought of picking up the brush again?" Salt asked him.

"Afraid not," came the reply.

"You should, you have a special talent," said Salt.

Although pleased by what he heard Benson was perplexed by such a personal plaudit coming from a man whose compliments were a rarity.

"Nice of you to say so sir," he said.

"Time keeps marching on Benson," said Salt, "time keeps marching on."

"But I have encouraged my daughter to enrol at the art college," he told his boss.

"There doesn't seem to have been any children here," said Salt, while studying the family snaps on the sideboard and noting that Lizzie White's husband looked much older than his wife.

After a brief look through the rest of the house Salt asked Benson to organise forensics and two of the team to go through every drawer and cupboard and note anything of relevance. He also stressed they leave the property exactly as they found it. The two of them exited via the kitchen and after locking the door Salt asked his sergeant to return the keys to the young constable while he stood looking down a garden that was as immaculate as the inside of the house.

Beyond the lawn and the well pruned roses a perfectly shaped willow was just about to leaf and he suspected she had planted it to create the view before him now, with the willow taking the eye on to the distant woods that were still leafless and bare.

The woods that were a haven and a heaven and a playground for two kids who would run to it from the old farm. Run to it as fast as they could past the cottage of Clubbie, who would stand at its garden gate glowering at them. Old Clubbie with his six-inch black boot and his shiny well-worn black coat and his bald head. Old Clubbie the ogre who would one day surely strike them both dead. An old man who now attracted his sorrow knowing he had lived all his life in that cottage. Never married. Never moved on. Never smiled. But perhaps if they had smiled at him, he would have smiled back.

A heavy dew made it look like it had rained but It had not. The lifting clouds allowed a glaring sun to melt away the morning mist and shine its golden light upon the grass and the foliage and the early daffodils around the base of the willow, adding a million sparkling diamonds to a glinting scene that had no fiscal equivalent. From the wood came that seasonal song he had not heard for so many years but still divined a mood of gladness and hope and new beginnings and an awareness of looking beyond the obvious.

When the cuckoo calls.

Chapter Three
Gillian Turner

St Cuthberts held a special place in the hearts of the people of the town. Whatever the beliefs of those who had built it some seven hundred years ago they had still crafted a song into a structure that sang to all who entered. A song that greeted every visitor who walked in through its ancient doors with overtures of peace and well-being and comfort, cocooning them for the duration of their visit in a hushed atmosphere of wonderment and awe, laid centuries ago but still prevalent in a world of planes and boats and trains and moon landings. Erected with a built-in foreverness that still assured the troubled mind that time will heal and all is well. Salt glanced yet again at its inspiring spire and promised himself a visit but for now his own mind was elsewhere and The Blue Room beckoned.

There was an air of expectancy from the four who had gathered at his request. Except for the girl they had all worked together before but not as a team. It was her first day as a detective. A day she had longed for and looked forward to. Being in uniform had brought its rewards but it had its limitations. Now, here she was, realising an ambition that had come earlier than expected. The three men chatted amongst themselves. Not ignoring her but not knowing how to respond to her presence. She sat at her desk pretending to arrange papers while taking in their chat which was normal blokey stuff until the bald one furthest from her started adding crude innuendos that were not only meant for her ears but also meant to embarrass, and with each lewd comment came a self-congratulatory guffaw along with a glance to his peers for expected approval. But the approval did not come and she sensed that their embarrassment was deeper than hers.

Benson entered the room with Salt behind him. She had seen neither man before but guessed that the tall, still good looking J.F.K. type sporting a similar hairstyle was her boss. After Benson had finished pinning photographs and other details on to the board Salt turned and faced the four.

"We have a murder," he said, "and therefore we have a murderer. We have a mindful, inquisitive,artistic eighty-three-year-old who has had her life snatched away and I want to know why and by whom."

"We are still awaiting the P.M," he continued, "but I am almost certain her neck was snapped by someone skilful in such practices. This was not a random killing or a burglary gone wrong. Of that I am convinced. I believe she was targeted and cruelly dispatched by a professional who knew how to cover his tracks. Yet we have no motive and so far, no clues. There lies a difficult road ahead, so alertness is crucial. Looking for the unexpected is crucial. Now you may think that the suggestion of a contract killing in our backwater is rather far-fetched but I believe it to be true."

He also thought that his potential for peering beyond the provincial would not necessarily be shared by those listening to him and wondered if he had aired his views too early. Benson was aware of his boss slipping into a sphere that saw him thinking on his feet and talking as much to himself as to them. He had seen it many times before.

"Maybe the cluelessness was a clue in itself about it being a professional killing," he said. "Maybe not ransacking the place or leaving any evidence of a break in only goes to corroborate my thinking. His callousness knew no bounds but maybe it will be his undoing," he said, knowing in his own mind that the perpetrator was male.

Benson took over and with his school-master cane pointed to the first photograph on the board.

"Our victim is a Mrs Penny Campbell," he said, "who lived, as far as we are aware a quite ordinary every day existence in her little terraced house at the bottom of Stepping Street. As the boss has already indicated she was a talented lady, shown by the pencil drawings carrying her signature along with the artistic flair that echoes all through the house."

"Why have two photographs up of her?" asked the girl.

"Because she was an identical twin," answered Salt. "The other is of her sister, a Mrs Lizzie White, which may have no relevance whatsoever, but could be a factor we should all keep in mind. She was a widow and lived alone, the only other relative we know of is a brother who resides with Mrs White. We are not aware of any children," he added, and then apologised to his sergeant for butting in and motioned to him to carry on.

"We need to dive into every aspect of her life in the next few days," continued Benson and started dishing out orders to all four, "Crockett," he said, aiming his eyes at the bald one, "I want you to investigate her finances with a fine toothcomb highlighting any oddities that may be relevant."

Crockett nodded and brought his hands from behind his head that had been there for the duration of the meet and reached for his glasses and his pen and starting making notes.

"Yorke," said Benson, turning to the tall thin one just to the left of Crockett who had been standing leaning against the wall with his arms folded. "We want you to go back to the house but this time go through every cupboard and every drawer and every nook and cranny and read through every document and take note of every photograph looking for anything untoward."

"Will do," said Yorke and continued leaning against the wall waiting for the meet to finish.

Benson then turned to Edwards with his bespectacled professor appearance and asked him to come up with any contacts who had passed through her life in recent times while keeping aware that some might lead to others going even further back.

"In other words, a potted history of her past," said Benson knowing that Edwards with his love of the historical was perfect for such a task.

"And Turner," he said, allowing his eyes to meet up with the girl for the first time. "I want you to return to Stepping Street and go knocking on doors. Neighbours can sometimes provide us with seriously good info and I particularly want you to give full attention to the ladies. OK?"

Turner nodded but there was a disappointed look about her that if not noticed by Benson was certainly picked up by Salt.

"OK let's get to work," he said and started to lead them out of the room, but Salt motioned to Turner and asked her to stay behind.

Once the others were out of earshot he asked if she was settling in and were there any questions, she wanted to throw at him. He recalled his own first day and feeling unsettled and out of place.

"And if it was difficult for me," he said, "it must be even more difficult for you."

"Why for me?" she asked knowing what he meant but wanting him to put it into words.

But Salt, who had detected a steely look in the bluest of eyes that did not somehow match the colour of her skin, decided to sidestep a possible confrontation.

"We have a good team here," he said, "Never be frightened to ask, everyone is approachable for any queries you may have."

She grimaced and rolled her eyes at the word approachable, hoping Salt had not noticed. But he had, and his inner perception guessed the reason for it.

"Now I know that Crockett thinks he's God's gift," he said, expecting acknowledgement without receiving any, "and can come out with some crude stuff but he's a good cop and quite harmless."

"Harmless to men, you mean sir," she replied with that steely stare holding his without flinching.

"I'm here to become a good detective," she continued, "and I know I can, but I won't take that kind of crap, and I think you should know that."

Salt did not return her stare but raised his eyes and pursed his lips and stroked his chin, aware that if the wrong things were said she would walk away and he did not want to lose such an obvious asset.

"How about if I have a word?" he said.

"No way," she replied, "I can look after myself sir. I have had to. But there are many women out there who cannot or who are afraid to rock the status quo. That does not apply to me. Sir."

He had seen her C.V. and knew about the commendation she had not flaunted at her interview and his respect grew with every second she stood in front of him.

"You have an injury," he said, while pointing to the plaster on the knuckles of her right hand and at the same time changing the course of their conversation.

"Well, it's not exactly an injury," she said without further explanation.

"Then why the plaster?" he asked, aware that the answer would only come reluctantly.

She paused, not knowing how he would react and not wanting to be ridiculed but also knowing he would not let it go without an explanation. He was not the sort she thought, while working out that he had a habit of wheedling the revelations of others but extremely coy about revealing his own. "I've had a cluster of warts that I could not get rid but I have an uncle who said he could make them disappear," she told him, but instantly regretted her explanation sensing it would only increase his curiosity and not dispel it.

"And what does he use to make these warts disappear?" asked Salt.

She hesitated a long time before answering and then said, "Mind over matter sir."

"Mind over matter?" repeated Salt.

"Yes sir," she said.

"So, he's some kind of faith healer," stated Salt.

"Absolutely not," said Turner, "that is actually a term he dislikes intensely."

"Explain," said her boss, "I'm interested."

"Well, he is into all sorts," she said, "he is into telepathy and tarots and astrology as well as astronomy. He regresses and reads the runes and…"

"He reads the runes?" said Salt while thinking about his touchstone.

"Yes"

"And has he ever read the runes for you?"

"Yes."

"And the outcome?"

"I knew I would eventually take this path," she said, "but wondered if this was the right time so I asked him to read them for me and he told me that my timing was perfect. But he also warned me about my path crossing with this tall silver haired sleuth whose bite was much worse than his bark but whose guidance could be relied upon. Sir."

With just the hint of a smile Salt asked her the name of her uncle.

"It's Garman," she told him.

"And what's his Christian name?" asked Salt.

"That is his Christian name," she answered, "his side of the family had a tradition of giving their offspring out of the ordinary names."

"And which side of the family do you spring from," he asked, and immediately regretted his question while wishing the ground would swallow him up.

But she knew that there was an unthinking innocence about his question and felt sorry about his obvious embarrassment while at the same time being thankful that she was being addressed on his level and that his levelling up meant he looked beyond the colour of her skin.

"My mother should have been an American G.I. bride," she told him, "But he got posted before that could happen and she never saw or heard from him again. The family did find out that he returned to Tennessee and contact was made while he was still in the army but he did not reply, and after he was demobbed, he became untraceable."

"I often wonder if I have any of his traits," she added, "other than the obvious."

"My grandmother had a similar experience," said her boss, "the difference being that the man was already married with a child. My mother would think the same as you and always wanted to know about her father but it was kept from her and she went to her grave never finding out.

After she had gone a long-lost cousin emerged and told me he had played piano at the Scala for the silent films but did not know anything else about him. I also wonder if I followed my real grandfather in any way."

"What seeds we sow," she said, almost to herself, but just loud enough for Salt to hear. "What seeds we sow."

After their unintended revelations there was an awkward silence between them before Salt broke that silence.

"Right then, D.C. Turner," he said, standing up from the edge of the desk he had been half perched upon with his hands in his pockets. "We had better get you off to Stepping Street. Go and speak to the desk sergeant about having a Panda car from the pound and if you have any doubts about going it alone speak to him also about organising a P.C. to accompany you."

"That won't be necessary," she said, "I'm happy to go alone."

"That's OK," he said, "but do not enter any of the houses, regardless. If you think a deeper interview is needed then speak to me or Benson. I repeat, do not enter any property."

"I will not sir," she said with a solemn nod of the head.

"Just one more thing. We always try to work from our strengths. Now ladies, talk to ladies. If I were to send Crockett with his outlandish charisma and his dashing good looks those same ladies who would chat all day to you could find themselves tongue tied in the presence of such beauty," he said, accompanied by the broadest of smiles, "Now off you go."

"Point taken, sir," she said, and along with a smile that matched his own turned and headed for the corridor she would frequent for many years to come.

He watched her confidently walk away carrying an obvious smartness that had already gained his admiration and silently wished her well through the many difficulties he knew she faced.

From his pocket he pulled out his talisman and rolled it around in the palm of his hand thinking of her uncle and hoping one day to meet this man who had travelled a similar path and might possibly have come across the same words.

> *The sword was set in stone and not in sand,*
> *its drawing came through knowledge born of light*
> *and not the lesser power of the hand.*

Chapter Four

The Watch

As she swung into Stepping Street, she dwelled on it coincidentally being her first patrol as a young uniformed P.C. to it now being her first outing as a plain clothed Detective. She thought of patrolling with Sergeant Renshaw showing her the ropes as he put it, and how his mentoring and guidance over the years had contributed to the confidence she now felt. She remembered having doubts cast upon her youthfulness only for the doubter to told by Renshaw that she had an old head on her young shoulders. Mostly she cherished his professionalism in his helpfulness towards her which could not be said of others whose sinisterness was obvious. Now she had Salt carrying out a similar role. She felt blessed.

Up until reaching the home of Gail Shepherd, the young detective only received positive feedback regarding the victim. Yes, she was reserved, some said, the sort of person you never really got to know but she was always pleasant and approachable. Some even accepted that she seemed a cut above themselves and could not understand why she had not moved on from an area that was quickly becoming a magnet for the first-time buyer who was using the street as a stepping stone to their next purchase with no intentions of imbibing the communal spirit that had always existed before. None of them had been invited in but were pretty sure she kept the house updated because of the number of tradesmen that turned up at regular intervals.

"They were always going on holiday," said the neighbour who shared the same entry, "three or four times a year for two or three weeks at a time. But she would always knock on my door and tell me when they were going and when they would be back."

"Any idea where they went?" asked Turner.

"I sometimes inquired," said the neighbour, "but she would say just travelling. Of course, all that stopped when Mr Campbell died"

"And when was that?"

"I'm afraid I don't have a head for dates my dear, but not too long ago."

"Did she ever ask you to keep an eye on things?"

"No, but her sister would call round just to pick up the post and that, she was a twin you know."

"Yes, I know," said Turner.

"The first time I saw her sister I thought they had returned early. I could not tell them apart."

Turner thanked her for her time and assured her that there was nothing whatsoever to worry about when the woman raised concerns about something like that happening in their street, she then gave her a card to call her or the station at any time.

"We also have a constable stationed outside the house," she told the neighbour.

"And a lovely young man he is too my dear," came the reply as Turner smiled and wished her well then crossed to the other side of the street to knock on the door of the house opposite.

She thought the girl was about seventeen or eighteen when the door eventually opened and looking into the cold hard hostile eyes facing her guessed she was in for a difficult interview.

"My name is Detective Constable Turner," she said politely, while offering the girl a view of her warrant card which was completely ignored.

I am a loser here on three fronts she surmised. I am a copper. I am a female copper. And I am a black female copper.

"First of all, can I ask your name?" said Turner, turning towards her notepad with pen in hand.

"You can but you won't fucking get it," replied the girl and then asked the young constable what she was writing in her book.

"I am writing that you refused to give me your name," came the reply and she told her that they were making enquiries about Mrs Campbell from the house opposite who had died in suspicious circumstances and that they were questioning every householder to find out if they had seen anything suspicious or had anything to report that might aid their investigation.

"I don't know fuck all," said the girl while this time emphasising the expletive and looking for a reaction but getting none.

"I did not like her and she did not like me," she continued. "In fact, she was a stuck-up old cow."

"And what makes you say that?" asked Turner.

"Because she was," said the girl, "ask anybody up the street"

"Most of them only have good things to say about her," said the detective constable.

"And that's because they're stuck-up old cows as well," came a reply.

"Do you live here alone?" She asked the girl.

"What's it to you?" was the answer that came back.

"Because I would want to talk to them also." Said Turner.

"He knows no fucking more than me," said the girl, again with emphasis on the swear word.

"And who is he might I ask?" said Turner.

"None of your business," said the girl.

"It's very much my business young lady," said Turner, adding a sternness to her statement. "We have a neighbour of yours who was quite possibly murdered and I have every right, if you decide not to co-operate, to escort you down to the station where you will be…"

"He's my grandfather," the girl cut in, not wanting to go to the station.

"It's his house," she went on, explaining that it was a temporary arrangement and that as soon as she was back on her feet she would move on.

"And what is the name of your grandfather?"

"It's Colin Shepard."

"And you are?"

"Gail Shepard"

"And is your grandfather at home Gail?" asked Turner, with what she thought was the patience of a saint.

"No, he's up the bookies," she answered, "then he'll go on to The Jockey and get back sometime this afternoon."

The running nosed child, who Turner guessed was about three years of age, seemed to come from nowhere and stood at Gails side staring at the stranger on their doorstep.

"Your daughter?" asked the detective.

Shepherd only nodded but nodded reluctantly. The child then reached and tugged at her mother's mini-skirt before holding up her arms to be picked up but was told to go back into the fucking house.

And so, it goes on, thought Turner.

But still she found a tinge of sympathy for a girl who should have been furthering her education or out with her mates or serving in some store or even being deafened in the stamping shop at the chain works. Instead, life had stamped its own ring of steel around Gail Shepherd.

"Well thank you for your time," said Turner "If you do think of anything perhaps you could ring me on this number."

When Gail reached for the card Turner took note of a watch on the girl's wrist which had been hidden by the defiant folded arms covering it.

"Nice watch," she said,

"Its ok," said Gail and quickly resumed the defiant stance.

"A present?" asked Turner.

"What's it to you," came the reply.

"Just wondered," said the detective.

"If that's all, I've got to go," said the girl and turned and slammed the door.

The watch bothered Turner. Should she investigate while the image was still fresh or continue knocking on doors? She decided on the former.

The town had three jewellers with the oldest and most reputable being Mannion's, so she decided to visit that one first. After failing to identify a watch like it in the window she entered the shop to be greeted by a smiling young man of about thirty wearing a smart grey and pink striped seersucker blazer sporting a pink carnation. His almost matching tie sported an extremely neat Windsor knot stemming from a stiff white collared shirt while a neatly pointed handkerchief of the same material sat in the top pocket of the blazer.

"Can I help you madam?" he said along with the warmest of smiles.

"I hope so," said Turner, while at the same time producing her warrant card which he took in his stride as though it were an everyday occurrence,

"My name is Patrick," he said and offered his hand.

She took it and started describing the watch she was trying to identify. He gave a rather puzzled look until she said its brand name could begin with an overlarge italicized capital B with the rest of the letters arched beneath the minute dial.

"Ah," he said, "we are talking about a Benenzo," and motioned her towards the back of the shop where a free-standing cabinet displayed just three watches.

"The one on the left," he said, "is obviously a ladies watch while the one on the right is meant for the male of the species and the one in the middle can be for either."

"That's the one," she said pointing to the middle of the three.

"Well, I'm glad I have been of some use," said Patrick.

"And what is the cost of such a watch?" asked the detective, noticing they carried no prices.

"Well think along the lines of a Rolex," he said.

"I have no idea how much a Rolex like that would be, Patrick," she informed him while stressing that such luxuries were way out of reach of the average copper.

"Well, that particular watch retails at around three thousand seven hundred pounds," he told her.

"Wow! Absolutely beyond our pockets," she said.

"And how many do you tend to sell?" she asked, followed by, "Not too many I imagine."

"More than you think," he said, and went on to explain how they were the only local franchise and that people came from within a radius of about twenty miles to order one, "People have to order them?" Said Turner. "You mean they can't just come in and buy one."

"Oh no," Patrick replied, feigning an astonished look, "We are talking Rolls Royce here Miss Turner. Each one is made to the customers specification, I mean the gubbins is mostly the same except for the amount of gold or diamonds one wants to pay for but no two faces are identical and each one is numbered. The price I have given you would be for the basic one on display but even that would have to be ordered. We carry no stock."

He was chatting away now like the ladies on the doorsteps, giving her a brief history of the watch and how the company is still owned by the same family dating back to seventeen fifty.

"A bit like ourselves," he said, "I am a fifth generation Mannion and proud of it."

"So, you should be" said Turner, and asked if he remembered any local buyers in recent times.

"The last locals to buy was about two years ago when a certain couple came in and ordered one each. Some sort of anniversary as I remember."

"And the name of the couple?"

"Now, Miss Turner," he said, "I think you know that I cannot...."

But before he could finish, she said she entirely understood his need for confidentiality but this was a murder inquiry and if he was not prepared to divulge the information asked for, she would come back with the necessary paperwork that...

Now it was his turn to intercept and with a not so friendly tone explained how a Mr and Mrs Campbell were regular clients buying not just jewellery but also the occasional fine China figurine the shop was also famous for displaying.

"Then as I say about two years ago, they came in and ordered the watches, one for him and one for her," said Patrick, "but she went for the middle one rather than the ladies."

"And were they personalised?" asked Turner.

"Very much so," replied Patrick, "each watch was initialised in gold on the back. She had wonderful taste, and although I cannot remember without referring to our records exactly what they specified I do remember he paid us round about eleven thousand pounds in cash so their requests must have been quite substantial."

"In cash?" repeated Turner, "without questions from you?"

"What is there to question Miss Turner," said Patrick, but now with a more business-like attitude. "It is an everyday occurrence for us."

"So, when can I see your records?" asked the young detective.

"I will have them ready by ten tomorrow," he replied, and then went on to tell her that since Mr Campbell had passed away his wife had been in to have his wedding ring altered to fit her own finger.

"Thank you for your time and trouble," said Turner, "I will call back tomorrow."

"Can I inquire if this is connected with Mrs Campbell and if she is ok," Patrick asked.

"You can, but I cannot answer that question," came the reply.

"So, I have to answer your questions but you will not answer mine," he shot back at her.

"I'm afraid that's the way of the world Patrick," she replied, and turned to walk out of the shop but not before taking time to study photographs of the five generations of the shop owners framed up on the wall, with Patrick's being the last one on the right.

"No, that's the way of your world," said the jeweller rather coldly as she went out of the door.

She found Salt at a desk in The Blue Room with his coat on the back of the chair, his sleeves rolled up, and his glasses balanced on the end of his nose reading reports and making notes.

"Sorry to disturb you sir," she said, "but I think I have stumbled across something I think you should know about."

"You can disturb me any time from this," he replied while motioning to the paperwork, "but shouldn't you still be in Stepping Street?"

"I still have about half to do," she said, "but decided this matter needed investigating."

Looking up at her over the top of his glasses Salt listened intently as she reported on the events of the morning and after she had finished took off his spectacles and placed them on the desk and sat silent for a few seconds before speaking.

"That's good work Turner," he said, "that's bloody good work."

"Thank you, sir," she replied in a matter-of-fact way that told him she had no intention of milking his praise.

"We bought our wedding rings from Mannion's," said Salt, almost to himself as he rotated his around his finger before shaking the thought from his mind and asking her the names of the girl and the grandfather.

"Their names are Gail and Colin Shepherd," she told him.

"Shepherd?" said her boss. "You did say Shepherd?"

"I did sir,"

"Colin Shepherd?"

"Yes sir"

"And how old was this Colin Shepherd"

"I did not get to meet him sir but I would imagine around your age."

Salt stood up and went to the window and looked up to the three sycamores lined about twenty feet apart in the distant hedgerow. Trees that they would approach from the ten-acre field after running like mad under the murder bridge. Standing now like three leafless sentinels silhouetted against a flinty sky. He remembered how the two of them would sit and lean against the middle one smoking the smoke wood they experimented with after cutting it from the hedgerow and recalled making sense from nonsense as they righted the wrongs of the world.

"Now what the Christ have you been up to Colly?" He said to himself, but loud enough for Turner to hear.

"You know him sir," she asked.

"I knew him." He said, and then went on to tell her how they had grown up together, and gone to the same schools together, and delivered newspapers down Stepping Street together, but did not tell her about a reputation that had reached him even in London.

"We played in those fields," he said with his back still to Turner. "Made bubble pipes from the cups of acorns, robbed the nests of birds, and shot at them with our catapults but always missed. No watches for us but we always returned home in time for tea."

I hope to Christ you are not involved Colly, he thought, with his mood matching the impending sky and threatening rain. I hope to Christ you are not involved.

"Is he there now?" asked Salt.

"No sir," said Turner, "Gail told me he would be back after his drinking session at The Jockey.

Sometime between three and four."

"Right, its two thirty now," he said and suggested she went off to the canteen for a bite to eat and a coffee and to meet him in the car park at three forty-five.

****

Well at least I was wrong about the cladding, thought Salt, as they pulled up at the front of the house with the offending property being further up on the opposite side.

"This used to belong to a Mr and Mrs Hall," he told Turner while still sitting in the car. "Mr Hall was deaf and dumb. Naturally I just thought he was born that way but I was wrong. They had a daughter named Rachel who was about my age and an older son named Anthony who I never saw. Anthony went off to war and was captured by the Japanese and came back just skin and bone. But they were glad just to have him back. So many did not return. A week or so later Mr Hall opened the door into the bathroom not knowing his son was stripped to the waist washing himself at the sink, and seeing the scars on his back from the many lashings was struck dumb.

He also lost his hearing. Two weeks later Anthony committed suicide."

"Not a nice story," she said.

"The world at that time was full of such stories," he said, as they exited the Rover and took the path up to the front door.

Salt allowed Turner to reach for the knocker and as she did so he noticed that her knuckles were free of any blemishes.

"Your warts have gone," he said in mock astonishment.

"Of course, they have," she replied, while managing a smile and a sideways nod of the head along with raised eyebrows that asked why he should think any different.

After opening the door Gail Shepherd raised her own eyes skyward and asked what the hell, they wanted this time.

"Is your grandfather back?" asked Turner.

"He's asleep in the back room," answered Shepherd.

"Then we better come in and wake him up," said Salt.

"And who the fuck are you?" she asked with as much venom as she could muster.

"This is Detective Chief Inspector Salt," said Turner as he brandished his warrant card.

"He's asleep," she repeated.

"Well, either we wake him or the squad cars will with all sirens blaring. It is up to you." he said.

She opened the door to allow them entry and led them into the back room while telling her grandfather that the police had arrived. Turner entered first and found her grandfather lolling in an easy chair very much wide awake with a can of beer in one hand and a cigarette between two fingers in the other watching the horse racing.

"Mr Shepherd," she said, "As your granddaughter has probably told you we are making inquiries about the death of your neighbour opposite and wondered if you would mind answering a few questions."

Shepherd remained in his chair while telling Turner he knew nothing and had seen nothing so there was no point in the conversation going any further. He had just finished talking when her boss entered and stared down into the eyes of his old friend who looked up into his and with a disbelieving stare and a shake of the head said.

"Well, if it isn't the cigarette saint himself."

"Looks like you've had your fair share today Colly," said Salt, ignoring the obvious and intended provocation.

"I have my fair share every day Salty," he replied while adding as much sarcasm as he could muster to his old friend's name.

"But what the fuck's that got to do with you," he continued, and swigged again from the can.

"Because I can hear the beer talking and…"

"Oh yeah, and what would you know about beer talking," said Shepherd cutting in, "I don't suppose you ever got pissed in your life."

Salt then caught the eye of his constable and nodded after taking his stare from Colly to the watch and then back to her.

"Miss Shepherd," she said, instantly picking up on her boss's lead, "perhaps you would like to tell me how you came by the watch you are wearing?"

After glancing down at the watch Gail looked with pleading eyes at her grandfather and then told Turner she could not remember how she acquired it.

"Well can I tell you, "Said Turner, "that that watch belonged to Mrs Campbell and unless you can come up with a valid explanation as to how you come to be wearing it, it will be my duty to arrest you in connection with the…"

"I gave it to her," blurted her grandfather.

"And can I ask how you acquired it, Mr Shepherd?"

"I bought it from this guy in the pub," he replied.

"And can I ask the name of this guy?"

"He was just some guy selling stuff," said Shepherd. "You know how it is; you don't ask no questions and you don't get no lies."

"And this was at The Jockey?" asked Salt.

"Yes" said Colly answering too quickly and realising immediately that he had set himself up.

"So, if I take myself off to The Jockey," said Salt butting in, "and ask whoever serves there now, along with your drinking buddies, they will remember this guy and how you purchased the watch from him."

Shepherd stared long and hard at his old friend and then switched his gaze to Gail before putting his empty can on the table next to him along with the others already emptied and stubbed out his cigarette in an ash tray before putting his head in his hands.

"I'm waiting Colly," said Salt, knowing he had him cornered.

"I came back from The Jockey that night, "he said, while addressing the floor rather than those in the room. "And noticed there were no empty bottles on the doorstep and stupidly thought she had gone away without cancelling." He then paused and took a deep breath before painfully continuing. "I've noticed her recently placing a key under a pot in the porch and there was no one about so I went across the road and I found the key and went in."

Only the chime of a mahogany mantle clock sitting on a sideboard just to the right of Salt broke the awkward and embarrassing silence as Colly struggled to carry on with his confession.

"I was standing just inside with my back to the door ready to go back out because I knew I had done something stupid, when," and he paused again, "when some car headlights coming down the street lit up parts of the room, and I spotted this watch placed by a photograph of her husband on some sideboard just to the left of me and I picked it up and put it in my pocket."

Turner shot a quick glance at her boss but only noted a serious stony expression.

"Then I turned," said Shepherd, "to walk out just as more headlights lit up the room and that's when I saw her and saw those eyes, the sort of eyes I saw so many times in Korea and I kind of knew that she had gone."

"But I didn't kill her Salty," he went on, while taking his pleading gaze from the floor to meet those of his old friend, "I swear to God Salty, I did not kill her."

"I know you didn't," said his old friend with compassion turning to anger over the predicament he had been placed in.

"Fucking hell Colly!" he said, and shook his head and slammed his fist against the door which, being ajar carried his punch and softened the blow.

"I can't let this go Colly," he shouted, "I cannot let this go."

"I know you can't Salty," Colly cried, "I expect everything…"

But was cut off in mid-sentence as the door leading to the stairs in the left-hand corner of the room behind the television creaked open, and the child came in dragging an old teddy and eyed every adult before standing at the side of her mother and reaching up with her other hand which her mother took.

In the awkward silence that followed Salt saw himself sitting on the stairs in his blue striped pyjamas listening to the beer talking garbage his father brought in from pub and which his mother had to endure on a regular basis. He remembered descending the stairs one time and opening the door into the kitchen where they were drinking tea. "Why don't you leave my mother alone." He nervously said to his father. Only for his father to cradle the cup in his big hands and crush it so that bits of crockery and tea and blood fell to the linoleum floor. "That's how much I care," said his father. "That's how much I bloody care." His mother then picked him up and carried him back to bed and tucked him in saying that she was alright and not to worry.

Breaking the silence, and his own thoughts, he then found himself telling Shepherd that he wanted him down the station at ten in the morning when he was sober to be officially interviewed by Detective Constable Turner. He wanted him to repeat everything he had told them and sign the statement, to which Shepherd nodded without speaking.

"I can't let this go Colly," he said again with a saddened voice.

"I know you can't," came the even sadder reply.

Salt then motioned for them to leave and Turner walked out of the room first before being followed by her boss who had stayed behind taking one last look at a scene, he wished he had never witnessed.

"I never did get pissed you know Colly." he said, "Never, not once. I could not," but his old friend was not listening and did not answer.

They sat in the car without words and she sensed he wanted time alone, so she took herself off across the road to the constable standing guard and chatted to him and others coming and going from forensics before returning.

"We used to come carol singing down this street," he said, after she returned and settled. "Colly and me and Pete and Stinky and Georgie Trevis, who was the toughest girl you ever came across."

Turner was not sure if he was talking to her or himself.

"We were dead scared of her so when she asked if she could join our gang, we were all too frightened to say no. Boy could she scrap. She was a warrior."

"Sometimes we got called cissies for having a girl along but Georgie would take them on and pummel them to the ground and kick the hell out of them until we pulled her off. They never called us cissies again. And of course, they never snitched. How do you own up to being beaten by a girl?

It was a different scene in the snow," he went on. "There was a warmth to it. What with flakes floating past the old street lamps and settling on the distant steeple and people opening the glow of their houses to us and handing us the pennies I am sure we did not deserve. In fact, we must have been bloody awful. None of us could sing and none of us knew all the words to the carols. but we all finished the figgy pudding song with gusto and felt good about ourselves."

As he turned his head towards the house they had just left, he told her how Rachel would come to the door with her father and how he always had a big smile for them as they butchered their renditions of Silent Night and Good King Wenceslas. He would even give them a sixpence which was more than anyone else in the street.

"Mr Hall would try to talk to us," he said, "but we could not understand him."

"Now just before I left for London," he went on, "I bumped into Rachel in Millets and Mace and she told me she had lost her father. Naturally I offered my deepest sympathy because I knew how much he meant to her. In fact, how much they meant to each other. Then I asked her why on earth he was so generous when he could not even hear us."

'Because you reminded him of Anthony going off carol singing with his mates,' she told me. 'He loved happy memories about Anthony.'

"I asked her if she remembered her brother but she did not. Then we kind of hugged and wished each other well and said our goodbyes, but just before I reached the door she shouted."

'Perhaps it was a blessing in disguise.'

"And when I turned with a puzzled look," she said. 'That he could not hear you.'

There were a thousand and one questions Turner wanted to ask this complexed man sitting beside her but knew that now was not the time. Perhaps there never will be a right time, she thought, and even if there was, I wonder what kind of answers I would get.

After a long awkward pause Salt started the car but could not set off down the street without picturing two ragged arsed kids with their baggy grey school socks down to their ankles putting their arms around each other's shoulders and walking off into those cinematic sunsets of their Saturday morning heroes.

The way that we were
makes the way that we are
and the way that we are
shows the way that we were.

Chapter Five

The Journey

Through likening each new case to an enforced unexpected journey, Salt had already decided that they were embarking upon a long and complicated trek. Most were simple day trips done and dusted with little trouble, but this one he sensed was an odyssey in the making, an excursion into the unknown. A litany of red herrings, he suspected, lay ahead, along with the blind alleys and cul-de-sacs and one-way streets such cases brought. There were many roads to take before reaching that distant goal of retribution for those having their lives destroyed by an act of barbarism. Why should any human being, he would say, have their personal journey cut short in such a way? Every killing, was, to him, an abomination, especially the pre-planned one.

Many a seasoned traveller rated the road along the way to be more important than the destination, but for Salt it was a necessary slog towards a justified journey's end.

The Blue Room lay at the opposite end of the station to his office, and from one window it was possible to look down into the arboreal beauty of the town's park where Mary and he would meet after work during that first glorious summer together. Meeting then, with the flower beds ablaze with colour and the trees in full foliage and the cormorant and the heron in statuesque mode at the edges of the pool waiting for their next meal, while the mallards and the occasional swan and the Canada geese peacefully shared their environment with the moorhen and the coot.

He remembered the cute little tufted pochards arriving every year during the first week of December and loving their presence until leaving always during the last week of February. What of their timing and their journey? Where did they come from and go back to? Even when visiting his parents at wintertime he made a point of going to see them.

It was Crockett who entered first for the briefing with the others eventually following to be met with a nodded greeting from Salt. Benson arrived last carrying a sheaf of papers which he placed on the desk in front of the board before looking across to his boss for affirmation that he could start, and after stroking the fingers of his left hand through his hair and down to the nape of his neck looked up and addressed the team.

"OK" he began, "We all know why we are here, and I am aware I have your reports on the desk but I would like each of you in turn to verbally give an account of your findings so far, as sometimes the shared collective along with questions and inputs can reap dividends. Turner, perhaps you would start."

Whether or not he had thrown her in at the deep end or thought an early baptism was better than nervously waiting her turn she did not know. But she did know that competence mattered more for her than for the others and with a short pause and a look into the eyes of all around, gave what she thought to be a full and conclusive account of the events of the previous day.

"That's good work mate," said Yorke in his usual laconic manner and then turned to Salt to ask him if he was sure of his old friends' innocence.

"Absolutely," replied his boss, "He is not capable of carrying out such a killing. If she had been knifed or strangled my suspicions would have remained high but a professional job is beyond Colin Shepherd, believe me, we must look elsewhere."

Like a terrier unearthing truffles Crockett had a knack of nosing where it mattered. Give him a forest of figures and if an anomaly existed, he would sniff it out. His foraging of the fiscal often highlighted irregularities the majority would miss.

"It's early days yet, "he said, while standing to air his report, "but I can confirm that the Campbells lived a very much cash-oriented existence which kind of falls in line with D.C.

Turner's account of them paying for the watches in pound notes, so to speak"

"What amounts are we talking about?" asked Benson.

"Don't know yet," replied Crockett, "but just the one account accessed so far, and I know there are more, shows them receiving regular cash payments of five hundred to a thousand pounds most months despite being both retired."

"The source of the payments?" asked Salt.

"Can't say that yet Sir," Crockett answered, "but I sense someone knows how to cover tracks."

"And are those payments right up to present time?" asked Edwards.

"No" replied Crockett, "they stopped with the death of Mr Campbell."

"What of the other accounts?" Turner asked him.

"At least two," he said, with a fixed stare into her eyes which she met until he looked away. "This one account shows transfers between all three," he continued, "but access won't be available until I get authorisation."

"And when do you expect that?" she asked.

"Within two days," came his reply.

"Thank you" said Benson, then nodded at Yorke, who seemed to wait an eternity before moving to his desk and opening his folder.

"There is something odd about this house," he said. "It is immaculate throughout with all kinds of expensive stuff spread about including paintings and etchings and antique maps and porcelain figurines that most certainly did not come from Woolworths, but evidence of them living there for the last thirty or so years is virtually non-existent. No passports, no receipts, no bills, or diaries or any of the kind of mementoes other than photographs. It is most weird."

"Perhaps I have an answer that might explain," said Edwards interrupting his colleague. "For although they did not advertise the fact, they also had a rather nice property in North Devon."

"No one mentioned that to me," said Turner, "not even the next-door neighbour who told me about their many holidays. Maybe that is where they went every time."

"And maybe they did not like neighbours knowing they had a second home," said Yorke, "but that could tie in with the keys I found in a kitchen drawer that had Combe Bay written on a tag attached to them."

"Isn't that an area familiar to you?" Salt asked Benson.

"Yes, we holidayed there many times with my parents and later with our own children," he replied.

"And do we know what they did for a living," asked Salt.

"Yes, they were both qualified accountants, "replied Edwards, "but it seems she had not worked for years. He had worked for a large international called M.K.P.T before retiring."

"Maybe when I get to talk to her sister, we can start to interweave a few threads." Said Salt.

"And when do you expect that to be Sir?" asked Benson.

"Tomorrow morning," Salt told him, "She has a brother living with her who I have been in touch with and he tells me she should be OK by then. I was going to take you with me but I suggest that you and Edwards shoot off to that address in North Devon with that bunch of keys."

The two men looked at each other and nodded and both said they were able to go.

"It's a good journey there and back," Salt said to them, "so take some overnight stuff just in case, you might be an hour at the house or you may be three or four, and remember to have a word with the local force before entering the house."

"Will do," said Benson.

After thanking his team Salt went over to Turner and asked her to accompany him to Mrs White's before returning to his own office just as the phone was ringing.

"Salt speaking," he said into the receiver but received no reply.

"Salt speaking," he repeated, and waited.

After several seconds a voice said, "It's Colly"

There was a long pause from Salt before he just said, "Yes?"

"I remembered something," said his old friend.

"About what?" asked the detective.

"About my time in the house."

"And what do you remember?"

"I remember the smell of after shave." Said Colly.

"You remember the smell of after shave?" Salt asked.

"Yes." Said Colly, "and I also think he was still in the house and maybe I disturbed him."

"You remember the smell of after shave and you think you disturbed him?" said Salt.

"That's what I said," came the reply."

"Even though you were pissed out of your mind?" said Salt sarcastically."

The sound of the phone being slammed down shocked Salt who realised immediately that he was out of order and dialled back but his call was not answered. It took three more for Colly to pick up again.

"I owe you an apology," said Salt.

"Sometimes you can be an arrogant bastard," said Colly.

"I've said I'm sorry," said Salt, and carried on talking hoping to defuse the situation and get his old mate on side again. "So how do you think the after shave could be important when there are thousands of brands around?" he asked.

"Because Stinky used it and he always said it was an exclusive one." Colly explained.

"So, you are telling me that Gordon might have been involved," said Salt.

"No, I'm not saying that at all, he could not have been anyway, he's dead."

"Stinky is dead?" said Salt in an unbelieving tone, "Stinky is dead?"

"Yes," said Colly.

"When did he die?" asked Salt

"About two years ago," Colly replied.

"How?" asked Salt.

"Car crash," replied Colly.

"And no one bothered to let me know," said Salt.

"You mean like you used to let us know what was going on in your life after you left. Not once did you bother to contact us. Even when you came back to see your mom and dad. You were seen around but you…" and he trailed off not wanting to widen the already obvious chasm that was building between them.

"And you are sure about the after shave?" asked Salt.

"Yes, I am sure,"

"How can you be so sure?"

"Do you remember Miss Fontaine?" asked Colly.

"Of course," said Salt.

"And the scent of her perfume when we walked into her classroom?" said Colly.

"Yes," said Salt.

"And if you stood next to a lady today using the same perfume today, would you pick up on it, even all these years later?" Colly asked him.

"Point taken," Salt replied.

"When we asked about his after shave," Colly continued, "he would tell everyone it was bought in Austria and was manufactured exclusively for some Baron Von Clinkenberg, which of course was a pack of lies."

"He was a good liar," said Salt.

"We all have our faults," said Colly.

"And how does all that help me?" said Salt, ignoring the obvious insinuation.

"Because Kathy told me it could only be bought from one shop, and when he ran out, he had to send for it from there. Maybe your murderer does the same."

"That's good thinking," said Salt. "Now what about disturbing the culprit?"

"That I can't be sure of," said Colly, "but every time things come to mind, I hear a door shutting, and if that did not happen why do I think about it?"

"So how can I get hold of Kathy?" Salt asked him.

"You can always find her at The Jockey," replied Colly.

"The Jockey?" queried Salt.

"Yes," said Colly.

"You mean she serves there?"

"No, she owns it.

"Kathy owns The Jockey?"

"Yes."

"How come?"

"What do you mean, how come?"

"Well, is she the tenant or…."″

"No, she owns it, lock stock and barrel so to speak."

"Since when?"

"They bought it a couple of years before he died. It was always an ambition of theirs."

"How on earth could they afford to…."

"Christ Salty, is this some kind of inquisition. He worked bloody hard when he came out of the forces which you would not know about because you weren't around."

"I'll go and have a chat with her," said Salt.

"Yes, you do that."

"Thank you Colly, I owe you a pint."

"Yeah" said Colly and put the phone down.

The pub was not the pub he remembered. It was no longer the dour drab smoke-filled establishment frequented by his father and his father before him along with their expectation that he would follow in their footsteps but much to their disappointment he did not. To see two young ladies in mini-skirts up at the dartboard when he entered brought memories of the female of the species only ever entering the snug. That is except for the occasional one who would come storming into the bar with her husband's dinner and slam it down in front of him scattering the dominoes and cribbage board while reminding him he had three kids at home who had forgotten what their bloody father looked like.

The room bore no resemblance to the dingy working man's conclave of yesteryear. It was light and airy with pastel green painted walls and a brilliant white ceiling with its downlighting replacing the nicotine stained one of days gone by. The old worn shabby seating had now been reupholstered with a green tartan material that followed through on to the chairs beside the light oak tables. He particularly liked the photographs and drawings of the old town on the green pastel walls adding a homeliness that never existed before.

Kathy was pulling pints from one of the many pumps lining the counter whereas once there was only a choice of two. Mild or bitter. Now there were half a dozen different ales with almost as many lagers. After topping off the beers she placed them in front of the two young men sitting on bar stools who he guessed were the boyfriends of the girls. He made his way to the other end of the counter as if waiting to be served. Unlike Mary she had allowed her hair to go grey but he could still see that vivacious girl his mate had been attracted to all those years ago. It was not until she finished serving that she turned and saw him.

"Samuel Salt," she said, "Samuel bloody Salt."

"Hello Kathy," he said.

"I heard you were back, how's Mary?"

"She's fine, but not so glad to be back."

"Then why bother?" she asked.

"Sometimes life takes you where it wants you to be Kathy," he said.

"Forever the bloody philosopher," she said. "doesn't seem like you've changed."

"I'm sorry to hear about Gordon," he told her.

"Who let you know?"

"Colly."

"So, you two have been in touch."

"Yes."

"I'm sorry," he said again.

"It is what it is," she said, then offered him a drink.

"Coffee will be fine." he said.

"Still no booze?" she asked, to which he replied with a shake of the head.

"Gordon loved a pint," she said, "but he did not live for a pint."

"Unlike Colly," said Salt.

"Unlike Colly," she repeated, "who is most definitely not a teetotaller."

"Neither am I," he said firmly, "I am not a label, Kathy."

"Even as one of the lads," she said, "you never indulged."

"I had my reasons," he replied.

"Reasons you have no intentions of sharing I suppose," she said.

"Why should I?" he asked.

"It's called talking, Samuel," she said, "it's called opening out."

"You mean like sitting at a bar downing seven or eight pints and talking gibberish." he said.

"You know that is not what I meant." she said.

"There's another world out there Kathy," he said, "the world of music and poetry and art and going home to your wife without being stoned out of your mind."

"There is also a world of people, Sam, friends and colleagues and mates. Gordon loved those things also but…."

"But what Kathy," he said cutting in, "what are you saying?"

"I'm saying that," and then she paused, "that maybe we set off on the wrong foot."

She then looked at him long and hard and was unsure about carrying on with the conversation but he started to tell her about Collie's revelations.

"You know he's not such a bad guy," she said, defending their old friend but he ignored her comment and asked about the after shave.

"Gordon loved nice things," she said, "he hated run of the mill stuff and wanted difference. Not to show off or to prove anything but just for himself. That is the way he was."

"And the after shave?" asked Salt.

"We were in Salzburg," she said, "for his fiftieth, and we came across this little store selling custom made perfumes and fragrances and after shaves and I bought him a bottle for his birthday. The bottle was in the shape of a violin. It cost a small fortune."

With the memory obviously affecting her she paused and composed herself before continuing.

"That same night we went to a concert where they played The Clarinet Concerto which you introduced him to and got him into classical. I can never listen to it now without…"

But her words trailed off and tears welled before slowly running down her cheeks. Salt offered his handkerchief but she turned his offer down and pulled a pretty one of her own from the sleeve of her blouse and dried her tears and dabbed her eyes.

"He thought the world of you, you know Samuel" she said, "and was hurt when you did not keep in touch, but he always made excuses for you. 'That's the loner in you him he would say.'

"I loved him too, Kathy," he said with a seriousness that let her know he meant what he was saying. "As I did with Pete."

"You had a funny way of showing it," she said.

"I never forgot any of you Katherine," he told her. "Sometimes you move on and before you know the years have fled and…"

"I'll fetch the after shave," she said, before he could finish.

In her absence he looked again at the way they had transformed the place and congratulated her on her return, but she took the congratulations without comment and placed the bottle of after-shave and a card containing details of the store upon the table.

"I won't need the bottle," he said.

"You are not going to get it," she replied, and unscrewed the top and held it under his nose.

"That's some smell," he said, then picked up the card and stood to leave but did not do so without giving her a hug and offering her again his deepest sympathy.

"Make sure you give Mary my love," she said.

"I will," he replied.

"How on earth she puts up with you I'll never know." she said, along with a smile.

"Somebody has to," he replied, returning the smile.

"We had some good times you know Samuel," she said, "the four of us,"

"We certainly did," he said, with a saddened look, then turned and walked away.

Before reaching the door, it was pushed open and Colly came walking in. They both paused but passed each other by without speaking.

Kathy went back to her work and busied herself washing and drying glasses and rearranging bottles that did not need rearranging. The encounter had upset her and she felt glad that Gordon was not around to witness it. She recalled reading the words of some American writer saying we should never return and thought that maybe he was right.

Colly sat alone at the bar with his two hands around his tankard staring into his beer, wishing his old newspaper buddy had not come back. His homecoming had caused complications and he did not like complications. He much preferred the world that the drink would take him to.

Salt sat in the Rover looking up at a cluster of blackbirds gathered on a leafless elm, aware that his single mindedness was upsetting certain people but he had no choice. It was not his fault a murder had occurred on his return and that the killing had connections with people he had known. He was still here, living and breathing, but because some cold-blooded bastard had decided he had the right to end her existence upon this planet Penny Campbell was not. A passing car backfired and suddenly the blackbirds were gone, except for one, who for some reason, started to sing.

Until the road is taken
the journey can't begin.

Chapter Six

Keramos

Their drive to the house on the hill and the arranged meeting with Lizzie White meant passing. One Way Wood and Clubbie's cottage and the old farm where he was born. It was a road he had not taken since leaving for London. The frosted ferns and fences and fields and leafless boughs brought praises from them both. Salt often thought of the wood as a custodian for those cherished childhood times when they played in a place no grown-ups could enter. When immortality reigned and the mysterious was accepted without the need for explanation. When giants and aliens and ogres of every kind lurked behind every tree waiting to pounce. They were memories he would rekindle when trying to disassociate himself from the cynical and sinister world he had to inhabit in London. From the scenes that sickened but no longer shocked. Not for him the romantic Agatha Christie crimes that lacked reality and the devastation heaped upon close relatives which he had to witness and deal with.

"It's quite an amazing morning," said Turner.

"I'd forgotten how such a morning can affect you," he replied, "the city sometimes immunes you from such beauty."

"It's a strange name for a wood," she said, "how did it come by that?"

"No one knows," he replied, "just one of those hand me down things we take for granted, but I suspect it's to do with hamlets and villages being linked by footpaths and there being only one way to them through the wood."

"Is it the same one you can see from Stepping Street?" she asked.

"It is" he said, and then went on to tell her how they would play there as children, making dens and playing the sort of games that boys play.

"So, you had a friend around here?" she said.

"He was actually my uncle," Salt told her. "Who was the same age as myself, my gran had him late in life, we were like brothers. He lived on the farm my grandad kept just up from the wood. I was born there myself."

"Is that the gran who gave birth to your mother," she asked.

"Yes," he replied.

"Then he was not your real grandfather?"

"You are very astute young lady," he said, "but yes you are right,"

"So, you are a country bumkin at heart," she said with a smile.

"Not quite," he said, returning the smile. "My parents moved into a council house just the other side of town, but I would still spend weekends and school holidays on the farm.

After passing the wood they came to where Clubbie's house should have been but Salt was both shocked and saddened to find that it had gone. Replacing the old farm labourer's cottage was a large modern detached property surrounded by beautiful manicured gardens and an in and out drive upon which sat a Jaguar and a Mercedes. He stopped the Rover to take a closer look while telling Turner about the old man who had lived in that tiny dwelling from birth until death.

"Why did they call him Clubbie?" she asked.

"Because he was born with a club foot."

"What's a club foot?"

"It's a birth defect where the foot is turned inward and usually shorter than the other."

"I see."

"In Clubbie's case it was six inches shorter and he wore a big black made up boot."

"Not nice," she said.

"Not nice at all," said Salt. "It kind of defined him and his life. Never moved on, never married, most probably never even kissed a girl."

"Sad." she said.

"Sad beyond words," said Salt, "I can see him now dragging that six-inch boot."

He could not help but compare the apparent prosperity of now to the poverty of then. He left the car to stand for a while with his back to the house to take in the same scene that would have confronted Clubbie from his garden gate as those two boys raced past thinking he would turn them into frogs or strike them dead. He took in the hedge and the field beyond the hedge and the mighty gnarled oak still sitting in the centre of the field. A tree that was always begging to be climbed and often was. A tree for all seasons that saw Clubbie through every one of his.

Returning to the car he sat quietly for a moment with his hands on the steering wheel.

"We used to climb that oak," he eventually told Turner.

"You wouldn't climb it today," she said, "not covered in that frost."

"Clubbie never climbed it at all," said Salt.

"How old do you think it is?" she asked,

"Two hundred years at least," answered Salt, "possibly older."

"Never ceases to amaze me," she said, "for months they sit there leafless and bare looking dead,

then suddenly they come back to life."

"Springtime Resurrection," said Salt.

"Never heard it called that before," she said.

"It's a poem."

"A poem?"

"Yes."

"And that's the title?"

"Yes."

"I would like to read it, who wrote it?"

"A friend of mine," said Salt, "his name is Michael"

"Perhaps you will let me have a copy."

"I will."

"By the way what was Clubbie's real name?" she asked.

"I don't know," he answered.

"You never knew his real name?"

"No."

"So, you don't know if he was a George or a Robert or a Jack?"

"No, he was just there as we grew up and everybody called him Clubbie."

"That kind of takes away his humanity," she said.

"There was another man," he said, "we called Dirty Dick."

"Dirty Dick?"

"Yes, he lived in Mount Street in a little terraced house. I believe they have gone now."

"They were pulled down about ten years ago," she told him.

"So, you know it?"

"I know it well."

"He lived in a tiny terraced house which was dirtier than him. He always wore an ankle length long black grimy overcoat and he walked with slumped shoulders. He was not bald like Clubbie but his hair was long and grey and greasy and hung over his overcoat collar. I can see him now.

He was like something out of Dickens."

"Was he harmful?"

"Oh no nothing like that. Some said he was a casualty of the first world war, there were quite a few around in those days."

"You mean the old days," she said with a smile.

"Yes, Detective Constable Turner. The old days."

Although the village of Hill Church possessed a medieval church, that church did not sit upon a hill, which always struck Salt as odd. Driving through reminded him that his mother went to school in the village, walking the one and a half miles there and back each day from the farm.

Starting as a four-year-old and leaving ten years later to go out into the world of work. Half a mile on from the school, Black Bag Mill still had its wheel turning and several times a year opened its doors to allow visitors to inspect its ancient lineage.

The gated driveway up to Lizzie White's property was situated opposite the mill, and the gate was left open which Salt assumed was for his convenience. The steep, long, rhododendron lined drive took them up to the double fronted Edwardian house he still remembered. But the views it commanded across three counties, which was quite spectacular on such a morning had slipped his mind or was not taken in on that first visit. Before they could ring the bell, the door was opened and they were greeted by a tall angular man with piercing grey eyes that met them with an openness and a genuine warmth.

"My name is Robin," he said, "I am Mrs Whites brother."

"And I am Detective Chief Inspector Salt," he was told, "and this is Detective Constable Turner,"

"My sister is in the lounge and expecting you," said Robin, "so if you would like to follow me."

Salt also remembered the large oak panelled hall with its black and white diagonally tiled floor and high ceiling and ornately carved oak staircase and supposed that the various antique pieces and paintings it housed now were the ones he saw back then.

Robin opened the door to the lounge and ushered them in. Lizzie White was sitting in a winged armchair along with a long-haired German Shepherd sitting to the right of her and an occasional table to her left housing a decanter of sherry and a half full glass, the same as when he was ushered in all those years ago. She was wearing an exquisite navy dress accompanied by a three-strand cultured pearl necklace and her short grey wavy hair looked like it had been coiffured that very morning. Salt thought that she looked at least ten years younger than her real age.

Her brother introduced them and suggested that the two of them sat on a three-seater settee opposite his sister as he pulled out the stool of a mini baby grand piano and sat himself down with his arms folded and his legs crossed and pushed out in front of him.

"I'm afraid you have caught me at my tipple time again Detective Chief Inspector" she said, while emphasising his rank, "but there again I don't suppose you remember."

"Of course, I remember," he said.

"It's not as bad as it looks," she went on, "I have one now and one about nine in the evening."

"I also recall you had a German Shepherd then, baring his snarling teeth and scaring the living daylights out of me." Said Salt with a smile.

"He was just a pussy cat really," she said, smiling back, "but he had this complex about men in uniforms. As some of us do."

"How many such dogs have you had?" he asked, ignoring the innuendo

"About five or six I think," she told him. "I had my first for my twentieth birthday."

"Now Mrs White," he said in a more serious tone, "we would like to offer you our deepest sympathy over the loss of your sister and we are here to find out more about her and to assure you that we will do everything we can to deliver the justice she deserves."

"It almost finished me," she said, dropping her smile "and sometimes I wished it had. We were closer than close and in touch nearly every day. To lose her was bad enough, but in such a manner has kind of left me for dead."

"It's early days yet," said Turner, who moved up to the edge of the settee and placed her hand on top of the wrinkled hand of the older lady, "but as the days pass, I am sure she would want you to realise that her time here has passed, but yours has not."

The old lady then moved to the edge of her seat and while looking into Turners eyes reached out and softly ran the back of her hand down the cheek of the young detective.

"I used to be beautiful once," she said, "just like you"

"You still are Mrs White," replied Turner, and gently squeezed her hand.

"You did not tell me you were bringing an angel with you Detective Chief Inspector," she said, while Salt looked on, along with the realisation he was witnessing a coming together of two ladies that was beyond him.

"If you are not up to answering questions today," said Turner, "we can always come back."

The old lady leaned back in her seat and Turner did the same as her brother suggested that he could answer most questions but his sister hinted that she would be OK.

"We have a photograph of you and Penny standing next to army issue motorbikes," said Salt, "can you tell us how that came about?"

"It was taken during the war," she answered, "we were both couriers transporting documents between different command posts all over the country."

"What kind of information?" asked Turner.

"I don't really know," she replied, "it was put into locked panniers which we just handed over and sometimes we were given panniers to return with but not always."

"I am assuming perhaps, secret documents," said the young detective.

"We did not assume anything in those days D.C. Turner, you just did your job, which was not easy. Hurtling around the highways and the country lanes with no signposts to guide us, we very much had to keep our wits about us."

"And can you recall any odd incidents that happened to either of you?"

"Just the one," she replied, "Penny was once found unconscious at the side of the road. It was worked out from the scrapes on the bike that someone had collided with her and the bike slid along the road as did Penny who went headlong into a tree knocking her out. A passer-by came across her just as she was coming round. Luckily her helmet saved her from serious damage."

"And the panniers?" asked Salt.

"They were untouched. It was thought that someone collided with her on the wrong side of the road and scarpered."

"There was that odd incident at the American Air Base you told me about," chipped in Robin.

"Oh yes, I was asked to deliver documents to an American air base when I was stationed in Cambridge, with strict instructions to personally hand the panniers over to the Commanding General whose name if I remember right was Rossington, but upon arrival a Sargeant came from behind the barrier and told me I was expected and for me to hand the panniers over to him as requested by the General."

"And did you?" Turner asked her.

"No," she replied, "he then got quite shirty and refused to lift the barrier so I said I would go back and speak to my superiors and at that he lifted it for me to go through."

"And did you report this to anyone," she was asked again by Turner.

"Both to the General, who said no such request had been made and to my superior, but without explanation from either. It has always bugged me though, as to how that Sargeant knew about me arriving at the camp."

"And what did you do in the war?" Salt asked Robin, "while your two sisters were dashing all over Britain."

"I was a C.O." replied Robin without further explanation.

"A conscientious objector?" Said Salt.

"Yes," said Robin.

"He was also a medic and an ambulance driver and risked his life many times in the heat of battle," said his sister, "and spent two years in Dresden after the war helping to rebuild that obliterated city."

"You don't have to justify my actions Lizzie," said Robin, "not anymore."

"Can I ask where you were on the night that Penny lost her life?" Turner then asked him while looking down at her notebook.

"Of course, you can," he replied without any animosity whatsoever, "I was up in Cumbria at a meeting along with about sixty others. I did not return until the next morning."

"And can you let us have details about that meeting?"

"Of course," he answered.

Although Salt was slightly taken aback by her suddenly throwing in the unexpected question, he was also aware of being assisted by someone with the same instincts as himself as he watched her look up from her notebook and ask the brother what he had done for a living.

"I was an accountant," he replied.

"For yourself or for a company?" she inquired.

"I worked for a company called M.K.P.T." he told her.

"Isn't that the same company that your sisters husband worked for?" she asked.

"Yes, the same company as Robert" he said.

"And how did that come about?"

"That was through my husband," said Lizzie White, "he worked in finance and was familiar with many such firms but always said that M.K.P.T. was the best."

"So did you ever work on the same projects?" She asked him.

"No never," said Robin, "because of my German connections I was mostly based in Europe while Robert only ever worked domestically."

"Now can I ask you Mrs White, if you and your sister ever passed off as each other?" said Salt.

"Many times." Replied the old lady, "when we were schoolchildren and teenagers."

"But not during the war years or since?" asked Turner.

"Most definitely not," came the reply, "and I do not see where you are going with this, it seems to me you are just clutching at straws."

"Sometimes we have to clutch at straws to build haystacks," said the detective. "Perhaps your sister, for instance, was mistaken for you. Could you have been the intended victim?"

Although her boss had given Turner a free rein and understood her reasoning he was unsure about the last suggestion and the detrimental effect it might have but he need not have worried.

Lizzie White was not some fragile old lady.

"Then we shall have to give them a run for their money my dear," she said, "if that's the case."

Salt then decided to explain how her sister had died and how he thought it was a professional assassination and suggested a police presence at Moss House for the time being.

"I cannot imagine such sinister goings on in our family," she said to him, "it all seems a little fanciful and far-fetched to me."

" You would be amazed how often the fanciful and the far-fetched occurs," said Salt, and then went on to ask her why her sister had remained in Stepping Street when a better property was not beyond their means.

"Sounds to me you are being rather snobbish Detective Chief Inspector" she said, along with what Salt took to be a twinkle in her eye.

"Not at all," said Salt, "I am just trying to understand why…"

"Because Penny had created a home she never wanted to leave," she said, interrupting him, "I have a house here, but she had a home. They also owned a property in Devon which I am sure you are aware of but that was also a house compared to the home of her creation."

"I think we have taken up enough of your time," said Salt, "but before leaving we would like to thank you both for your cooperation under such difficult circumstances."

"Please come back any time," she said, "if you think of anything else you want to ask."

"We will," said Salt as he watched her stroke the back of the dog's head who gave her the kind of look that only dogs can give.

As they stood to leave Lizzie White also stood and took both Turner's hands in hers and thanked her for her kindness before turning her attention to Salt.

"Won't you have a sherry before you go," she said, while giving a smile that offered an insight into the vivacious young lady she once was.

"Better not," he replied, while returning an even bigger smile.

Before accompanying them out, Robin gave Turner details of his night away and thanked them for their concern but doubted a police presence was necessary with him being there, but Salt begged to differ and told him arrangements would be made.

Before getting into the car Salt walked to the edge of the gravel drive to look out across the still frosted hedgerows and meadows and fields and villages and church steeples that eventually took his eye to Malvern some twenty-five miles away.

"Elgar would walk those hills," he said, "and further over to your right is Brown Clee and the beginning of Housman country."

At the bottom of the drive, he stopped the car to take in a scene that never failed to impress him.

"To think that a wheel has turned at that mill for almost a thousand years." he said. "Serving a community that changed little over the centuries as the seasons came and went."

"Keramos," said Turner almost to herself.

"Keramos?" questioned Salt.

"It's a poem by Longfellow about the turning wheel of the potter," she told him. "My uncle often quotes from it. Turn, turn, my wheel. All life is brief. What now is bud, will soon be leaf."

"Now that is something I will have to read," said Salt.

"Make sure you do," came the reply.

The return journey remained silent until passing the wood again when she suddenly felt confident enough to say, "I think we have our man, Sir."

"I presume you mean Robin?" he said.

"Yes," she replied.

"And what makes you say that?" he asked.

"Dare I say instinct, Sir," she said, and waited to be admonished but was not.

"Instigator or perpetrator?" he asked.

"Instigator." She replied.

"And you think you can prove it?" he asked.

"I think the team can prove it in time," she answered, "we have a good team"

"Including Crocket?" he asked.

"Yes," she said.

"They both must go on the board as suspects," Salt stressed, "but suspects without personal suspicions, is that understood D.C. Turner?

"Completely, Sir," she replied, "but you mean Mrs White, as well?"

"Now just because she sees a halo above your head," he said, "it does not mean that she can be dismissed."

"I don't know what you mean," said the young detective.

"Oh, I think you do," said her boss, as he pulled into the station car park, "for it seems to me that you were both humming from the same hymn sheet."

There is a song the angels sing
that has no voice and needs no ear,
whose lyric is, a whispering,
to seeking minds and hearts who share,
their silent ministry.

Chapter Seven

The Breath of Jesus.

Knowing of his proficiency in extricating the wheat from the chaff, Salt hoped that Benson's trip to North Devon would harvest rewards. Monitoring the peripheries mattered, and he could think of no one better. Benson was nothing if not persistent. A student of detail and exactness with an ear and an eye for the shape beyond the shadow. Salt was deeply aware of his own career flowering because of the many seeds planted by the efficiency of his loyal sergeant.

Although they were only days into the journey the murky road ahead had not, as yet, shone a light on the reason or indeed the motive for the brutal killing of Penny Campbell. There were possibilities and suspicions, yes, but up to now no lamp in front of the carriage to guide them. Was it the brother as Turner suspected, or both him and the surviving sister between them? If so, why? Did the regular cash payments received by the Campbells equate to some kind of blackmail plot? The payments stopped after Robert's death. So, were they just to him without his wife knowing or to the them both? Did she have information about the instigator that could bring them down? Was Colin Shepherd involved after all or were the war years hiding a dark and sinister secret?

He had many balls to juggle but up to the present they were all up in the air.

After leaving Bridgewater and bypassing Stowey, which he was loathe to do, Benson branched off to the little historical harbour town of Watchet telling his companion that they would take the coastal route. At Watchet he paused long enough for Edwards to view the sculpture of The Ancient Mariner and informed him how the writer of the poem and his literary comrade had walked to the town from his cottage and how they had been investigated for being French spies. Edwards though seemed completely uninterested so they motored on to Blue Anchor Bay with its many caravan sites and a beach that stretched for miles with views across to Minehead where the distant flags from the holiday camp reminded Benson of a surprisingly good family holiday when he least expected it. They soon arrived at Porlock and after negotiating the infamous hill the road straightened out for them to take in the alluring sight of Exmoor being bathed in spring sunlight accentuating its curves and valleys.

"You are right about it being a brilliant drive," said Edwards.

"Glad you like it," said Benson while pushing a cassette into the player which brought the meditative lushness of clarinet and horn into the car.

"I always play this along this stretch of road," he told his companion.

"Sounds good, what is it?" asked Edwards.

"It's Beethoven's Pastoral," came the reply.

"I did not know you were into classical," said Edwards.

"Have been for years now," said Benson.

"I'm a Zeppelin fan, myself," said Edwards with a smile, as the mood of the music seemed to match perfectly with the rolling hills folding into a mysteriousness that was only available to those of a certain nature.

"I knew him going back," said Benson.

"Knew who?"

"Plant."

"You knew Robert Plant?"

"Yes."

"How?"

"By playing in bands."

"You played in the same band?"

"No, just other bands around the same time."

"Before he made it?"

"Yes."

"What did you play?"

"Bass," said Benson."

"Were you any good?"

"Why do you think I became a copper?" replied Benson.

His partner smiled.

"I would never have made it, but I remember him telling me he was determined."

"Wow," said Edwards.

"He was a really nice guy," said Benson.

"Never got into that scene myself," said Edwards, "even though I was given a guitar by an uncle who was a big Donegan fan."

"No Donegan, no Beatles," said Benson.

"No Beatles, no Zeppelin," said Edwards.

"All lanes lead to Lonnie," Benson suggested, while distorting the metaphor.

After a mile or so Benson pulled into the side of the road, switched off the engine and motioned to Edwards to look to their right. Standing on a ridge about fifty yards away stood three of the moor's wild ponies. All as still as a marble statues silhouetted against an azure blue with their heads bent low employing that equine mindfulness which seems to place them upon another plane. The scene reminded Benson of Salt's experience in The New Forest. An experience he had even talked about because of its impact upon him.

He had been sitting with his back against a tree one bright September morning watching sunbeams shafting down through autumnal foliage and sparkling on the slow flowing brook when he became aware of three wild ponies close by. One of them eased its way across and stood over him before bending its head and touching his cheek with its nostrils. It then took its head back and snorted over him so hard that he could feel the pony's breath upon his face. After snorting a second time the pony then made its way down to the brook followed by the other two and was suddenly joined by six or seven more, seemingly coming from nowhere. They were all shapes and sizes and different colours and gambolled about in the shallow brook for a few seconds before leaving the glade and going off in different directions. Benson remembered Salt telling him he had asked an Essenic friend whose beliefs revolved around the animal kingdom for his thoughts and was told.

"What you experienced Samuel, was the breath of Jesus."

"And did you believe that?" his sergeant had asked.

"I believe, he believed, what he was saying," Salt had replied.

"But did *you* believe?" asked his sergeant again. Only for Salt to pause for what seemed an eternity before saying.

"Sometimes magic happens."

They were now in Lorna Doone country and Benson informed Edwards how the little church at Oare where Blackmore had his heroine killed was just off to their left;

"My kid sister must have read that book at least twenty times," said Edwards, "as well as seeing the film as often as she could."

"You'll have to bring her down and show her around," said Benson.

"That kid sister is now thirty-five years of age with kids of her own," said Edwards, "she can bring herself down, anyway she has probably forgotten all about Lorna Doone."

"I doubt it," said Benson, "early books leave deep impressions, I have never forgotten a book my mother bought me called Pete and the Prairie People"

"Funny how we have found out more about each other in the last couple of hours than in all those years working together," said Edwards.

"Typical coppers leaving personalities at home while dissecting those of others," said Benson, followed by, "I never even knew you had a sister."

"And I never knew you were into Beethoven," said Edwards.

"Somebody has to do be," replied Benson.

Lynmouth was soon upon them and Edwards marvelled again at what he was seeing.

"If we were abroad people would be in raptures about it," said Benson.

"I am in raptures anyway," said Edwards.

"You will have to come back and explore." Benson told him.

"I will," came the reply.

"Take the old cliff railway up to Lynton and walk down to The Valley of the Rocks or stroll alongside the river Lyn up to Watersmeet. The whole area is a haven beyond words," said Benson.

"Sounds like you work for the local tourist board," said Edwards,

"I should be so lucky," replied Benson.

The driver decided that they should push on and headed out into the North Devon countryside with Edwards continually praising all that lay before him.

"We have enjoyed many happy holidays down here," said Benson.

"And I can see why," said Edwards, as they drove through the next village without stopping.

"They used to mine silver around here," Benson informed his colleague.

"Really?"

"Yes, and some of it went into the crown jewels."

"You should have been a history teacher as well."

"I should have been a lot of things," said Benson. Then swung up out of the village to take the twisting rocky lined road leading to Combe Bay, but before reaching the town slowed down long enough for Edwards to get a view of its historic harbour and the little chapel just beyond the harbour sitting on a rocky tor facing the sea, as it had done for over eight hundred years.

At the station they were greeted by a Sergeant Popplewell whose jovial and friendly manner they immediately took to. After inquiring about their journey, he informed them that they knew very little about the Campbells. Inquiries had been made after being told about her murder but it seemed they kept very much to themselves when staying at the property.

"Although we do have a local P.C. living in a police house just down from theirs," he said, "who passes the house several times a week but who tells me he has seen nothing suspicious since we were informed about her demise."

"What's his name," asked Benson.

"His name is Bychkov," answered Popplewell, "P.C. Mikhail Bychkov"

"Doesn't sound much like your local Bobby," said Edwards.

"That is exactly what he is" said the sergeant, "and a bloody good one, his father was a Russian refugee who married a lass from Scotland. I've arranged for him to meet you guys in the canteen in about ten minutes time"

"Thank you," said Benson.

"My pleasure," said Popplewell.

The young officer who entered the canteen and looked over to them did not match the person they expected to see. He was well over six feet with a mass of red curls above a boned angular face with piercing Paul Newman eyes. As he came across, they both stood to greet him. Benson introduced himself first and then Edwards.

"P.C. Bychkov," said the young man as they all shook hands.

"Thank you for your time," said Benson.

"I hope I can be of some help," said Bychkov.

"Excuse me for saying this," said Edwards, "but your name conjures different features."

"You mean I don't look like I have Russian blood," said the redhead.

"Exactly," said Edwards.

"And what does a Russian look like?" asked Bychkov while smiling at them both.

"Not like you," piped in Benson with an even bigger smile.

"If you are interested," he said, "my mother came from Bunessan, a village on the Isle of Mull,"

"You mean where Mary Macdonald penned her famous tune?" asked Benson.

"Absolutely," said Bychkov with an admiring glance.

"Something my mother is extremely proud of," he continued, "coming from the same village as Mary who only ever spoke Gaelic and whose simple tune eventually spun around the world."

"And your father?" asked Benson.

"Well, in the strange world that we live in, my mother's great grandfather was a Russian seaman from a ship that was shipwrecked off the island in about 1860, and because of that heritage she decided to learn the language, then while at university in Glasgow went to a party one evening and heard this young Russian refugee trying to make himself understood and went over and interpreted for him. That refugee was my father."

"Some story," said Benson, "I assume then that you are named after your father?"

"Well, no actually," he replied, "I have my father's surname of course but Mikhail was the name of my shipwrecked ancestor."

"And how did you end up here in North Devon?" asked Edwards.

"Because my father became a lighthouse keeper and he was offered a post on one of Lundy's lighthouses," he told them.

"Your story gets even more fascinating," said Benson "but I think we should get down to the reason why we are here."

"Of course," said Bychkov.

"Now your sergeant tells us that the property has raised no suspicions while you were going about your business," said Edwards.

"Not until just now." Said the young P.C.

"And what happened just now?" asked Benson.

"You will see when we get there," he told them, "that the property enjoys an elevated position overlooking The Bay a few miles out of town. Cut into the rock beneath it is a parking area for about four cars and then there are steps up to the house. I was taking the bend just before the house about an hour ago and after rounding it was immediately confronted by a Black Range Rover that I felt had just pulled out from there."

"Did you get its number?" asked Edwards,

"Of course," said Bychkov, "and I followed him until reaching the island on the main road where he turned right towards Braunston and I turned left to come down to the station."

"But you were suspicious?" said Edwards,

"Very much so," he replied, "especially when he shot away at first then slowed right down to obey the speed limits as if not to arouse suspicion."

"And have you checked out the plate?" asked Benson.

"Yes," answered Bychkov, "and it actually belongs to a mini that was stolen in your vicinity about two weeks ago."

Benson and Edwards looked at each other and without saying as much both realised that this journey might not be a wild goose chase after all and could be the break that often happens when least expected. It was decided that Bychkov would lead them to the house in his Panda and that they would follow.

The older detective had never experienced the out of season hush that seemed to emanate from the hotels and holiday parks and guest houses they passed on their way down to the front. Only a few dog walkers strolled along the prom with heads down not even looking out to sea, giving the closed cafes and amusements arcades and gift shops waiting for Easter an even ghostlier look. But the younger man was still impressed by the sheltered bay and the mile long sandy beach.

"I can see why you come here," he said to his sergeant.

"If the conditions were right there would be surfers out riding those waves," said Benson, "it is fast becoming a surfer's paradise."

"I can understand that also," said Edwards as Bychkov turned right to ascend a winding road away from the resort. After about a mile he pulled into the parking area of the elevated house he had told them about and the other two parked beside him. They had just left their cars to climb the steps up to the house when the young P.C. suddenly shouted, "That's him," pointing at a black Range Rover that had slowly driven past, "He was just going to pull in but saw us and drove on."

"Are you sure," asked Benson.

"Convinced," said Bychkov as he opened the doors of the Panda and more or less ordered them to get in."

"You'll never catch him in that," said Edwards.

"I know this road better than he does. Now get in," he said, with an authoritative tone that surprised them.

The engine screamed as each gear was taken to its extremity but Bychkov appeared calm and in complete control while manoeuvring the hairpins with dexterous hands that would not have been out of place in some mountain rally. He even had the temerity to give a running commentary as he dragged every ounce of speed out of the little car.

"There is no way he could come up here like this," he said as the rough and uneven rocks either side of them became even craggier. "And he did not know that he was spotted and that we would follow so we have the advantage, but we have to catch sight of him before he reaches the village at the top of the rise to see which road he takes out of it."

"If I recall correctly there are only two," said Benson. "Left across the coast road or the right one which takes you back round to The Bay,"

"You've been here before?" asked Bychkov.

"Many times." replied Benson.

"There he is," said Edwards as he craned forward between the heads of the other two from the back seat. Bychkov slowed as they reached the village with its grey stone church on their left and the popular little café on their right that nourished the holidaymaker before taking one of the many paths that led to spectacular views of the rugged coastline. At the corner shop and post office the Range Rover turned left along a mile tree lined straight with many of the trees bent by constant winds coming across the open countryside. Bychkov followed at the same pace as the Range Rover until it suddenly accelerated and started pulling away, he followed suit at first but then slowed. "He's getting away," said Benson.

"I don't want to panic him," said Bychkov, "At the end of this straight after the nasty bend is a built-up area with houses and a school and it's just about time for the kids to be coming out and if he takes that bend too fast with someone pulling out from the ice cream van that's usually parked on the right, we could have an incident."

The black car did not slow and they watched it take the bend at speed and almost immediately afterwards heard the screeching of brakes and a crunching metal on metal crash followed by two grating more crashes and a thud-like bang. Rounding the bend themselves they found a scene that the young copper had almost predicted. A white Ford Escort was embedded into the offside corner of the ice cream van and opposite two small concrete bollards placed to stop drivers from parking on a grassy area had been torn from the ground. Skidding tyre marks across the grass led to a fence that safeguarded people from the sheer drop beyond it and a broken-down gap in the fence pointed to the fact that the black car might have gone through it and over.

The three policemen quickly left the panda and went about their duties. Edwards approached the Escort driver and the ice cream man now standing beside their vehicles assessing the damage but found that although badly shaken neither were seriously injured. Bychkov went over to the children walking home from school who had witnessed the accident and suggested that they continue on their way, while Benson followed the skid marks to the gap in the fence and looked down the embankment to see the Range Rover embedded into an oak which had stopped it falling to the jagged rocks and the sea. Edwards heard him shout, "Christ," and joined him to see the trapped vehicle some fifty yards below. Benson suggested trying to get down to it but Edwards came up with an emphatic, no.

"You'll never keep your footing on that scree Sarge," he said, "and only end up in the drink after hitting the rocks."

They looked on as they saw the driver's door swing open and a blooded hand reach out to hang on to it. "He's trying to pull himself out," said Edwards.

"All the services have been sent for," said Bychkov as he joined them.

"I feel so bloody helpless," said Benson.

"You'll only end up killing yourself," said Bychkov, "we just have to wait until…" but stopped in mid-sentence as with the others he saw smoke coming from the front of the vehicle and petrol seeping from the ruptured tank and before they could express their fears the explosion almost knocked them backwards and a fireball shot up into the oak and a sky that had started to cloud over leaving the three of them stunned while staring mutely at the burning car.

Within minutes the screaming sirens brought all three services to the scene. Even Popplewell turned up, but only to remonstrate with his two visitors for bringing mayhem to his patch. Bychkov though, thought differently, yes, he was sorry for the guy in the car but loved being involved in what he saw as the bigger picture and wanted more of it and knew that his days in Devon were numbered.

Leaving the mayhem behind, Benson took himself off to the call box further along the street and put in a reverse charge call to Salt to report on the events of the day.

"Are you sure he is dead?" asked Salt.

"No one could survive that, sir," answered his sergeant.

"If it is as bad as you say any possible evidence would have gone also," said his boss.

"Absolutely," said Benson.

"So, none of you got a look at him?" asked Salt.

"Blacked out windows" answered Benson, and then went on to question whether this guy was involved at all or was it just coincidence and that maybe Bychkov had mis-read what he saw.

"A coincidence does not drive away from the police at breakneck speed," said Salt, "and anyway it all ties in with what we now know.

"And what do we know now?" asked Benson.

Salt then went on to tell him how Turner had returned to Stepping Street to resume her house-to-house inquiries and was verbally accosted by one of the older tenants named Marsh at the bottom of the street about how the police never dealt with his complaints.

"And what have you complained about?" asked Turner.

"About people parking in my spot," said the old man.

"But people have the right to park anywhere in this street," Turner told him.

"Everybody sticks to their own spots down here," ranted the old man, "and I ain't putting up with some flash bastard in his big black car pinching my spot and I told him so."

"And what exactly did you say?" she patiently asked him.

"Well, when he did it a second time," said the old man, "I told him if he did it again, he would come back to find his car in not such a good condition as when he left it."

"Now for anything improper Mr Marsh you might just get arrested," she told him.

"Oh, that's typical bloody police sticking up for shagging foreigners instead of their own kind. They can come over here and…."

"So, why do you say he was a foreigner?" she asked after butting in.

"Because of his accent" replied Marsh.

"And what sort of accent was that?" asked Turner.

"German," said Marsh.

"And how can you be sure it was German?" she asked.

"Because I fought enough of them during the war," said the old man.

"Is there anything else you remember about him?" asked Turner.

"Yeah, he was as bald as a badger and he stunk like a tom-cat," said Marsh.

"So, he got out of the car?"

"No, I tapped on his window and when he wound it down, I asked him what he was doing here,"

"And how did he answer?"

"He said he was waiting for a friend but I didn't believe him"

"Why not?"

"Don't know, just didn't."

"Did you see the car the night Mrs Campbell was murdered?" she asked.

"Not down this end," answered Marsh.

"You remember the make of the car?"

"Yes, it was a Range Rover and it was black and had them dark windows."

"I don't suppose you made a note of its number plate Mr Marsh."

"No reason to," he answered.

"Now finally you say he stank. What did you mean by that?"

"Well, you know the way these youngsters today splash this stuff all over them, it was that sort of smell. Can't stand it myself."

"Thank you, Mr Marsh," she said, while handing him a card and suggesting he contact them if the black car returned.

"If he tries to park here again, he'll get both barrels," said the old man.

"Not literally I hope," said Turner, along with a smile that was wasted as he cantankerously turned and stomped off mumbling to himself.

We feel the wind

but cannot see

the force behind

its faculty.

Chapter Eight

Timing

After Salt had instructed them to book an overnight stay and use the following day to tie up any loose ends it was Bychkov who recommended they use The Belvedere, and even in a world that appears to encourage coincidence it was a monumental one that brought the two detectives to the establishment that Range Rover man had booked himself into the day before. And even then, it was only a chance remark by the young chatty flame-haired waitress serving breakfast that alerted them to that possibility.

"They asked me to get in early for number eleven," they heard her say when addressing the older couple on the table next to Benson and Edwards. "So, I was here for six thirty for him to get away quickly and he has not even turned up. I laid his table in the window as you can see but still no show and its quarter past eight."

"Maybe he's still up in his room," said the lady, "I remember last year we were on a coach holiday in Italy and one morning this fella who was on his own had not turned up for that day's excursion so they went without him but when we got back, they found him dead in his room."

"No, you've got that wrong, Freda," said her husband, "it was the Austrian holiday."

"No Jack, it's you that's wrong," said Freda, raising her eyebrows and shaking her head, "we were in Italy and we were going to Pisa for the day,"

"Now I beg to differ," said Jack, "I remember distinctly we were…."

"He's not in his room," said the waitress interrupting, "Rita from reception has checked, in fact he has not been seen since he booked in and paid up front, it's all quite strange"

"Did he arrive by car?" asked Benson, as the two detectives looked at each other.

"Don't know," replied the waitress, turning to face Benson. "You would have to ask Rita,"

The two detectives again exchanged knowing glances as Benson moved his chair back and stood to turn and leave the dining room. He was just about to go through the door when he heard Freda say, "I'm telling you Jack it was Italy and I know I'm right."

Rita was taking a booking on the phone so he busied himself admiring the foyer of this old but beautifully kept hotel. His father had been a master builder so his admiration knew no bounds for the expertly carved woodwork and the Minton tiled floor and ornate plaster cornices with matching roses that faced you as you entered through the large stained glass panelled doors.

Bychkov had chosen well, he thought, and wondered if Salt would feel the same when endorsing their expenses.

"Sorry to keep you waiting sir," said Rita, "but we only run a skeleton staff out of season."

"No problem," said Benson, who had taken a liking to her when booking in themselves. "I just wanted to ask you about the man booked into number eleven who has not come back."

"Are you both coppers?" she asked.

"Yes," said Benson showing her his warrant card.

"Thought you might be when you mentioned Mikhail," she said.

"You know him well?" asked Benson,

"Everyone knows him," said Rita, "he's a bloody good copper, an asset to our community. He will be missed when he goes. Now what is it you wanted to know?"

"I didn't know he was on the move," said Benson.

"He isn't as yet," she said, "but he won't stop around here. Too ambitious."

"This guy," said Benson, "can you describe him to me?"

"Yes," she said, "he was a good three or four inches shorter than you, probably about five nine."

"You are a good judge of height," he said.

"He was very slim but his face did not match his body somehow, he had puffed out cheeks and a rather large pockmarked nose and he was bald and wore what looked like a diamond stud in his left ear and also used an extremely strong aftershave."

"You should have been a copper yourself," he said.

"I was," she replied, "until…" but did not complete her sentence.

"Until what?" asked Edwards.

"It's a long story," she said, while seeming reluctant to continue. "One you would not like to hear."

"Maybe I like a long saga," said Benson.

She had already decided that she liked him and felt comfortable in his presence but still thought long and hard before continuing.

"There was this detective sergeant," she began.

"You mean like me," said Benson, interrupting in a jokey kind of way.

"No not at all like you," she said without responding in the same manner. "This one was always coming out with sexual stuff when one of us girls was around. Mostly we ignored him but the more you ignored him the more explicit he became. One of the girls complained but was told it was just blokey stuff and not long afterwards resigned. Then one day I was standing in the foyer passing the time of day with a couple of uniform guys and he came in and looked across and shouted 'Yeah she's just about right for a threesome.' I think the guys were more embarrassed than me but we just ignored him.

She paused then and took a few deep breaths before continuing. "That of course egged him on and he came across and said, 'of course if you guys don't know what to do, I'll join in and show you.' And then he laughed like the idiot he was but was only greeted by silence."

She was now looking beyond Benson while recalling the incident. "By then I was raging but told myself to keep calm and I walked up to him with my face only about twelve inches away from his and stared deep into his eyes but he would not hold my stare and I could see that he was out of his comfort zone and that is when I calmly told him that his sort were all mouth and trousers and would not even know where to start. There was a slight giggle from the two boys and whatever game he was playing he knew he had lost which only made him more aggressive and then he looked me in the eye and as venomously as he could called me a bitch, and when I asked him to repeat what he had said, he did."

She was now recalling with an uncomfortableness that made Benson uncomfortable and he was beginning to wish he had not pursued the matter.

"So, I sucked up as much saliva as I could," she went on, "and spit into his face and at the same time brought my right knee up into his groin and he went down like a sack of potatoes."

Benson wanted to respond but did not know what to say.

"And then I heard the desk sergeant say. 'What the fuck Rita.' But he had not said. 'What the fuck Barber,' to protect me. So, I went over to the counter and placed my cap on top of it in front of him and placed my warrant card inside my cap and said, 'that's it sarge, you make sure you look after your own kind.' And walked out of the station."

"I'm sorry," said Benson.

"Why should you be sorry," she said.

"Because I am," he said. While trying to supress a feeling he had never felt before, not even prior to getting married. They had liked each other, yes, but there had never been the sizzle that seized him now. Maybe that is why it did not last, he thought.

"That bastard is now a D.I," she said. "A verbal rapist and they bloody promote him."

"We are not all the same," he said.

"No, but there's loads out there," she said.

"Things are changing Rita," said Benson.

"If you think that then you are burying your head in the sand Detective Sergeant Benson," she said, "now can I ask if you have a Barber stationed at your nick?"

Benson did not answer but his non answer justified her question,

"I take it you resigned and came to work here," he said, while trying to alter the course of the conversation.

"Well, yes and no," she replied.

"I don't understand," he said.

"Well yes I resigned," she said, "but then I went and bought this place."

"This hotel belongs to you," he said.

"Just after I resigned my father died and being an only one, I inherited everything. Not that there was a great deal, he only had a tiny terraced house and a small amount of savings but there was enough for a deposit on this place which was quite run down at the time and I got it for a good price."

"And turned it into something special," he told her.

"I like to think so," she said.

Sensing that his stare would betray what he was feeling, Benson was now finding great difficulty in holding the gaze of the dark brown eyes looking back into his.

"Now this guy, did he sign in?" he asked.

"Yes," she said, and turned the registration book around for Benson to see that he had signed in as E. Ulrich with an address in Munich followed by the make and registration of the car.

"We know the car reg is false," said Benson, "and probably the address is as well. Your waitress said he paid up front, can I ask how he paid?"

"Cash," she answered, "now can I ask what all this is about?"

"Too complicated to explain at the moment," he said, "but I can tell you that he died when he crashed his car yesterday."

"That crash up on The Torrs Road?" she asked.

"Yes," he said.

"They tell me he burnt to death," she said.

"I'm afraid he did," Benson told her.

"Jesus Christ," she said, "what a way to go."

Because of the respect he had already built for her and the wedding ring on her finger he knew he could not show even a hint of an approach despite desperately wanting to. Apart from the age gap he also suspected the last thing she would want is for a copper to make a pass at her.

"Now did he leave anything in his room?" he asked.

"Yes," she said, "just a holdall which is sitting on the end of the bed and a couple of books on the bedside cabinet along with a pair of glasses."

"Can I see for myself?" he asked.

"Of course," she replied, "as long as I can accompany you."

"Still a copper at heart," he said while smiling and nodding, "I'll just fetch my colleague."

Freda was the type who talked but never listened. Who relentlessly prattled on from one unrelated subject to another without seeming to draw breath. And it was Edwards this morning who had to bear the brunt of her verbal diarrhoea. Jack continued tucking into his full English without even looking up. The waitress winked at the detective and smiled as Freda seemed to address her ceaseless diatribe to the holiday poster on the wall behind him.

"That's Claire" she said, as the waitress walked out of the dining room, "only been here a short time, but a nice girl. Before her it was Rachel who treated us like family. Her husband was a skipper on one of those boats that takes you to Lundy, we went once didn't we Jack?" who did not answer, "but I was sick all the way back and said I would not go again. Of course, we used to come here even before Rita bought it, I used to say to our neighbours you should come with us and try The Belvedere but they never did. I bet you two are business men. I can always tell business men when I see them. Jack was a glass blower you know, all his working life, fifty-one years with just a paltry clock to show for it. I read in the paper yesterday that…."

But by now Edwards had switched off in the way that senses switch off when sleep descends. If she had looked at him, she would have known but she did not and carried on addressing the holiday poster. Benson came in just as Edwards was wondering where the hell he had got to and this gave him a reason to stand up and politely move on.

"Thank you for the chat," said Freda as he walked away.

"My pleasure," replied Edwards.

Rita unlocked and opened the door to a single room that was as thoughtfully decorated as the twin one they had shared and stood in the doorway with her arms folded watching the two detectives go silently about their work. While Benson set about pulling out drawers and opening the single wardrobe that were all empty, Edwards unzipped the holdall and started taking clothes from it. When he thought he had finished he parted the holdall to get a better look inside and sternly said, "Sarge," and nodded towards the bag. Benson came across and looked in and after exchanging serious looks with his fellow copper took a handkerchief from his pocket and went into the bag to retrieve an automatic pistol which he placed carefully upon the bed.

"Bloody hell," said Rita.

The two men gave her a brief glance before carrying on with their work. After noting that one of the books was a biography of Neruda and the other an atlas of the local area Benson went into the bathroom and emerged holding a violin shaped bottle of after shave while his colleague unzipped a pouch at the side of the holdall and brought out a notebook which he flicked through briefly before saying, "Sarge, I think you had better look at this."

Only ten pages of the notebook had been used and at the top of each one was a name and beneath the name information about the person followed by an address. At the bottom of each page was a date followed by a tick. It was coming across the name of Penny Campbell with the date being the day she died that made them realise what they were looking at, and finding the names of her husband who supposedly died of a heart attack and Gordon (Stinky) Talbot who supposedly died in a car crash confirmed their thinking. Only the tenth page did not have a date and a tick at the bottom, but it did have a name at the top, and that name was Samuel Salt.

"Christ!" said Edwards as the two men looked at each other,

"So, the boss was right," said Benson, "despite my doubts."

"Doubts about what?" asked Edwards.

"About a pro being involved," replied Benson, "we shall have to warn him."

"I think we should give that some thought before we do," said his partner.

"I don't know what there is to think about," came the reply.

"We must ask ourselves why he is on the list," said Edwards.

"I think the answer is obvious, they want him off the case."

"Not necessarily," said his colleague. "Think about it. There are three victims connected to the boss and the third one did not die until he was back in town."

"I cannot believe what you are suggesting," said Benson with an incredulous look.

"He could even be the Mr Big," said Edwards, "he wouldn't be the first copper to turn."

"And set a hit man upon himself?" scoffed Benson, "it doesn't add up."

"Maybe he doesn't want it to add up."

"I just don't get your drift."

"His name being on the list makes him look like an intended victim."

"He wouldn't put his own name on the list," said Benson, "that was Ulrich."

"All things are possible," said Edwards.

"I think you are up a gum tree," said Benson.

"But up a gum tree with a detective's mind," replied Edwards.

Rita looked on, along with the realisation that she also had a detective's mind, and although not fully clued up to their situation understood their reasoning and non-reasoning and an anger began to rise in her about the way she had been forced out of a vocation she was meant for.

Benson moved over to the window to take in the distant sea view and the green meadows and the rocky coastline while at the same time admiring the prodigious artistry of a gull and tried to imagine life upon the wing away from such problems.

"I understand your reasoning," he then said to Edwards after pulling away from the window,

"but I have to tell you that there is more chance of the Kalahari turning arctic than there is of Salt turning sour."

"Maybe you are right," replied Edwards, "but it was something that had to be considered."

"I am assuming that this Salt is your Boss," said Rita to Benson while feeling he possessed a sensitivity that appealed and drew him to her, a feeling she had not experienced for a long time but tried to dismiss when the guilt kicked in.

"You assume correctly," he replied, then went on to tell her that they would remove Ulrich's belongings and that the room would have to be closed temporarily to allow for forensics.

"It is only what I expected," she said.

Edwards exited the room to fetch a bag for the belongings which left the other two awkwardly not knowing what to say until he moved again to the window and started praising the views from the hotel.

"One of the reasons for buying it," she said, "it's a little out of the way up here but we get spectacular sunsets and customers love sitting out on the terrace after dinner taking them in."

"I can imagine," said Benson, along with the realisation that they were only making small talk while deep down they both wanted to say more but knew that they would not.

Edwards returned and within minutes they were in the hotel lobby with the bagged evidence and their own holdalls ready to depart.

"I'll take these to the car while you check out," he said to Benson, who paid the bill then thanked her for their brief but enjoyable stay.

"You'll have to come again," she said.

"I'll make sure I do," he replied, but they both knew he would not.

"Under different circumstances," she said.

"Absolutely," he said, then turned to walk away but before he reached the door he stopped and looked back and said, "Bye," while nodding his head just once.

"Bye," she replied, and did the same.

At the door he looked back again upon a face he never wanted to forget and to stare just once more into those sultry photographic eyes that turned him to jelly.

David Sylvanus Benson had fallen in love.

****

Finding the notebook was a game changer. Not only for them but also for certain forces yet to be informed that unexplained deaths upon their doorstep may not have been as natural as they seemed. "Looks like we have ourselves a Jackal," said Edwards, as they left the hotel car park for the drive to meet Bychkov again at the house owned by the Campbells.

"And someone who knew how to contact a Jackal," said Benson.

"Might mean involving Interpol," said Edwards, "with the other six victims being in Europe."

"But I don't think they are connected to our case," said Benson.

"I agree," said Edwards, "looks like he was free-lancing and just went wherever he was wanted."

"Well, this killer will kill no more," said Benson.

"I also found it difficult to believe the boss when he talked about a pro killing," said Edwards,

"but there again the boss is a law unto himself."

"I said that to him once," said Benson.

"And how did he react?"

"He just said, I know Benson, but harnessing that law is another matter."

"And what did he mean by that?"

"Who the hell knows?" said Benson with a faraway look.

"I hope you don't tell him about my suspicions," said Edwards.

"I'm a detective first and an idiot second" replied his colleague.

"Thanks," came the reply.

"Nothing to thank me for," said Benson, who told him that such thoughts had even passed through his mind and if Salt had been in their position, he would have taken the same stance.

"What do you think of Turner?" asked Edwards suddenly.

Benson glanced briefly at his partner wondering what had brought on such a question then told him he thought she would make a good detective.

"I wasn't sure at first," said Edwards, "but now I only see her as an asset to the team."

"If she is allowed to be," said Benson, and then related Rita's experience.

"That's tough," said Edwards, "first losing her vocation and then her husband."

"Her husband?" questioned Benson, "how do you know that?"

"The forever talking Freda, at the next table," came the answer.

"When?" Asked Benson.

"About three years after she took over The Belvedere," Edwards told him.

"How?" Edwards was asked.

"Northern Ireland," came the answer, "he was a soldier."

"Bloody hell," said Benson.

"Are you interested then sarge?" said Edwards.

"Interested in what?" asked his sergeant.

"In Rita" stated Edwards.

"Definitely not," replied Benson, as he wondered why fate had timed their meeting if nothing was going to come of it.

After shaking hands with the young Constable, the three of them climbed the twenty-nine steps up to the large double fronted Georgian property that would have given them distant views across the Bristol channel to the Welsh coast on a clear day. The visiting detective's half expected to find the same homeliness as at Stepping Street but surprisingly opened the door to a beige, bland, almost minimalist décor that contrasted sharply to the warmth and the artistic style of the other property. Even the few paintings that did adorn the plain walls appeared to them as meaningless abstracts on unframed canvases and the kitchen only added to the coldness with its all-white units and Carrara marble worktops and splashbacks. Everything that could be chrome was chrome, including light fittings and door handles and wall sockets and legs on the sparsely placed furniture. Neither Benson or Edwards were impressed but Bychkov thought that the house had the wow factor.

"To get to this from what it was would have cost an absolute fortune," said Benson, whose knowledge of building practices told him that every wall had been stripped back to bare brick and re-plastered and false ceilings added to the high rooms.

"It's over-spending on a massive scale," he went on, "not the sort of dosh you dish out unless you have an endless supply. They would never get their money back,"

"A classic case of spending someone else's money," said Edwards.

Bychkov offered his assistance and after briefing him about their reasons for being there the three of them went quietly and methodically about their business, opening drawers and cupboards and wardrobes looking for anything untoward. Any documents they had expected to find in Stepping Street they found here in clearly marked envelopes. They even came across receipts for the two watches and all work carried out at the terraced house but none for their seaside getaway.

"Cash. No questions asked?" said Benson to the other two as they reunited in the kitchen.

"That would not be a problem around here," said Bychkov, and suggested he could supply them with names addresses and phone numbers of most of the tradesmen who had worked on the property.

"That could be useful," said Benson as they watched the young man go to the inbuilt micro wave and open its door and bring out what looked like a diary.

"What made you go there?" asked Edwards.

"Just had a feeling," said Bychkov, who then placed the diary on the worktop and started flicking through it.

"Dates and times," he said, while letting the other two look. Mostly the dates were at monthly intervals at Culbone and Porlock Wier, both places that Benson knew well. There was even one for that day at Culbone with the time scheduled for three thirty.

"Thinking of keeping that date sarge?" asked Edwards.

"We could make that before we head back home," he replied.

"But there is no one from here to turn up," said Bychkov.

"I know," said Benson, "but we must keep it. We have no choice. Keep it and see what happens,"

After choosing which documents to take back with them and suggesting to Bychkov that he keep the keys should they need him to go back in, the three of them descended the steps back down to the cars to say their goodbyes.

"He's a good kid," said Edwards, as they drove away. "We were lucky to come across him."

"Maybe it was meant to be.," said Benson.

"That sounds like a Salt statement," said Edwards.

"He has been known to make it," replied Benson.

"I don't buy it myself," said Edwards.

"If the time is right it will happen," said Benson with a smile that was caught by his passenger.

"It's all written in the stars I suppose," mocked Edwards.

"We may envisage the completed tapestry," said Benson, "but we still have to place the stitches."

"Well let's hope we stitch up the bastard behind these assassinations," said Edwards, while feeling clever about his response.

"Whatever will be, will be," said Benson with what he hoped would be the last word.

"Que sera, sera," said his friend, and as they topped the hill out of Lynmouth pushed the cassette into the player and said he thought he could get used to Beethoven.

"As long as you don't ask me to get used to Kashmir," came the reply.

Benson loved the way the word Culbone rolled off the tongue. Not only was it phonetically pleasing it also seemed the perfect name for an area of mystery and intrigue. Sometimes he would repeat it to himself over and over. No other place he knew conjured a need for an understanding of the unknown, especially when looking down on that tiny medieval church in a setting that could only be described as magical. None of this he mentioned to Edwards as they walked the two miles up to it from Porlock Wier. He was not a pious man, yet the path they took through those dense woods of sessile oak and sweet chestnut had, over the years, become like a pilgrimage. But he did tell Edwards about the Coleridge connection and how his old teacher thought that his most famous poem had the finest opening lines in the English language.

It was now three thirty and they were just beginning to believe they had wasted their time when two men emerged from the little church and walked between the gravestones while chatting before settling on the bench close to the iron cross. There seemed to be an altercation between them until the man wearing the Parka brought a package from his pocket and handed it to the one sporting a baseball cap. The detectives decided to separate and act like a couple of tourists with Benson entering the churchyard from the left and Edwards from the right. While Benson casually inspected the gravestones, even kneeling to inspect some of them, Edwards circled the church before seeming to take an interest in the iron cross as the men on the bench stood and shook hands and went their different ways. Edwards watched the baseball cap move towards the path that had brought them up to the combe and was sure he knew the man beneath it. His mannerisms and now his gait along with the slightest glimpse of his face convinced him. He walked over to Benson who was now peering through the leper window which allowed the afflicted to look in on a congregation being saved from their sins.

"The man in the baseball cap," he said, "is Patrick Mannion from the jewellers in the town."

91

There is no tick,
there is no tock,
no sands of time,
no cuckoo clock.

Chapter Nine

Jigsaws

There were those who believed that Salt's entrances were theatrical, and although his strutting confident manner along with his rasping Burton-like deliverances and his still obvious good looks added credence to their beliefs, they were wrong. Salt was not an actor, nor did he think, (despite the entertainment world building an industry around it) that there was anything theatrical or entertaining about the killing of another human being. Not everyone watched him stride into The Blue Room that morning to take his stance next to the information board but they all looked up when his stentorian intonations greeted them.

"As you can see," he said, "we have two extra bodies with us today, we have D.I. Briggs from the drug squad and D.S. Best from fraud, who are here because of material brought back by our two holiday makers."

"Benson Briggs and Best," said Yorke, "sounds like a super group."

Salt ignored the chuckles and pointed to a board that now sported more names and photographs and details, along with arrowing connections that gave it the look of a family tree.

"Because of our guests," he said, "I think we should recap and take stock after Benson has given us a full verbal of their two days away."

"We now know," he continued after Benson had finished "that we have three assassinations connected to this case. We have Penny Campbell, her husband Robert and Gordon Talbot, and I do not use the term assassination lightly. These three were targeted and a pro commissioned to kill them. Why? I should mention that I have, in the past, had associations with all three. Talbot was an old friend going back to my schooldays and the Johnsons I got to know briefly when I was a paper boy delivering their dailies."

"So, you really were young once," joked Yorke to a ripple of laughter.

"All the others are related," he then told them, "Or, have worked for the accountancy firm of M.K.P.T. Robin Dalton and Penny Campbell and Lizzie White are siblings with the sisters being twins. The late William White, Lizzie's husband, who died many years ago was also employed by M.K.P.T. and considered to be the catalyst for the others finding careers with that company."

"Did his wife work for that company?" asked Best.

"No" replied Salt, "she was many years his junior and did not work after they married."

"And Talbot?" asked Briggs.

Salt shook his head and went on to explain that he was in fact the odd one out and appeared to have no connections with the others or the company.

"And is the company under suspicion?" Best then asked.

"Not as yet," said Salt, "but I should point out that they had a branch in Dresden where Robin Dalton worked and the killer said he came from."

"And how do we know he was telling the truth, "Asked Briggs.

"We don't," replied Benson breaking in, "but that is what he entered in the hotel register."

"And has the address been checked out?" asked Crockett.

"It's false," said Benson looking across to his colleague.

"I have no knowledge of Culbone," said Briggs, "but I can tell you that several years ago Porlock Wier was used as a drop off point for drugs coming in from the continent but a sting operation put quite a few behind bars."

"Did that include the brains?" asked Yorke.

"No," he was told.

"So, he could have started up again," stated Yorke.

"Or she," said Briggs.

Salt looked on with a certain amount of pride as he witnessed his team inter-acting but then thought better of it when the wisdom of the old axiom kicked in. Detective work was a slog, a hard, mostly boring, behind the scenes slog, and those who entered its portals expecting to find a romanticized doorway into a world of glamourous excitement were quickly disappointed.

Along with an insight into the human condition that was not always flattering, the unheralded teams often slaved tirelessly and even sometimes put their own lives at risk in the line of duty for just one crumb of evidence. Returning home to the wife and kids was not always a certainty.

Dedication was the name of the game. As collator in chief, he knew he commanded a crew who would bring their crumbs to the table as conscientiously as any he had controlled before.

"I have a question," said Briggs while looking at Benson and Edwards, "why didn't you follow this Mannion fellow when he left Culbone?"

"Because," replied Edwards, "I had purchased several items from his shop over the years and although he appeared not to notice us when he was so involved with this other guy if we had followed him down the only path back to the harbour he might have turned and spotted me."

"We decided," said Benson, "that observance back home was the better option."

"And I had already interviewed him over the watch," chipped in Turner, "which was quite innocent and I am sure he viewed it that way but I can tell you that this guy has all his marbles."

"You may have noticed that I have also put my own name up on the board," said Salt pointing to his moniker.

"But without the fizzog" cracked Crockett.

"I have done that," Salt continued, "because of my many connections with those involved, something that I am sure raised suspicious thoughts with our two holiday makers when they discovered my name on the assassins list."

"No way," piped Edwards,

"As if?" said Benson.

"Well, I want you to be suspicious," Salt told them, "I want you to be suspicious of everyone and everything, to look beyond the obvious while at the same time realising that the obvious may be staring you in the face."

"We'll have him put away yet," joked Yorke.

"At least twenty years," said Crockett joining in with the banter.

" And I would still come out to run rings around you all," Salt joked back.

Turner looked on, admiring the way he went about his work. Admiring him for the respect he dished out while at the same time receiving it back in abundance. He may top the pyramid she thought but he knew he would not exist without the building blocks below. When the phone rang on her desk, she answered it then looked across at her boss, "It's Kathy," she said, "from The Jockey, she wants to speak to you."

Salt took the receiver and picked up the phones cradle and carried it over to the window and placed it on the sill as he looked down to the park with its abundance of daffodils and early leafing willows.

"Kathy?" he said.

"I need to speak to you Sam," she replied.

"About what?" asked Salt.

The others chatted quietly with each other or busied themselves at their desks.

"There is something I need to tell you."

"Can't you tell me over the phone?"

"I would rather you come over, if you can?" she said.

"Are you OK?" he asked.

"I just need to see you," she said.

"I'll be with you in about ten minutes," he told her.

"Thanks Sam," she said.

After telling Benson to carry on and report back to him later he left the station and was glad of the drive to clear his head about coming back to something he did not want but could not walk away from. The threads of nostalgia had needled a tapestry he now knew was just a pipe dream and he should have known better. People retire to their holiday destinations only to find that the roses are no longer around the door. He had returned to his home town only to find it was not the town he had left behind and neither were its people. They were locked away in a memory bank as he was with them. He had no wish to dissect and analyse and maybe even destroy those he had been close to in the past but the killings had taken that wish away.

Stinky, he knew, suffered from mythomania, he even recalled that time in The Galleon listening to him telling people that his father was in the marines while everyone knew he was in prison.

Telling them while Elvis, ironically, belted out Jailhouse Rock on the juke box. But his lying was accepted as a personality trait without it being questioned, in the way that young people accept each other's frailties. That is how he was, but being how he was did not stop him being a loyal and trusted friend and Salt felt that he was beginning to posthumously betray that friendship.

He also wondered what crime the father had been jailed for and if Stinky had followed in his footsteps. Had he fallen in with a bad lot? Did the lucrativeness of the drugs trade draw him into that murky world? If so, was Kathy aware? Was she going to suffer the same fate as Penny Campbell? The jigsaw was far from being finished and those pieces he expected to fit but did not were beginning to frustrate him in a way he had not been frustrated before. Maybe because he had come back with that vacation feeling of wanting everything to be rosy. Of not wanting to look beneath the surface and only seeing what he wanted to see. There were those in the force who made those pieces fit even if they did not, which to him was an abomination. He was no more a scene stealer than he was a cigarette thief.

When he walked into the bar Colly was sitting in his usual place and looked across as he entered but although their eyes met there was no word from either man. The only others in the bar were four men spreading dominoes at a round table and two ladies chatting over a drink. Kathy appeared to his right and gestured to him to follow her into her personal lounge. She had already placed pots of tea and coffee on the low glass topped table in the middle of the room and suggested they sat opposite each other.

"Coffee or tea?" she asked.

"Coffee, black, no sugar," he replied, then while she was pouring the coffee asked her again if she was OK.

"I've been threatened Sam," she told him.

"Who by?" asked Salt.

"They didn't say."

"What exactly did they say?"

"I was warned not to speak to you."

"Not to speak to me about what?" he asked.

"I don't know," she said.

"Kathy, you must know something they don't want you to talk to me about."

"I wish now I hadn't asked you to come."

"Well, you have, and I'm here, so tell me."

"There's nothing to tell," she said.

"Has someone contacted you after we talked earlier?" he asked.

"I've decided I don't want to discuss it Sam," she surprisingly told him. "Just forget I called you."

"You know I can't do that," he said.

"Well, that's tough," she said.

"So, there was a phone call and you were threatened," he stated.

"For Christ's sake Sam, please drop it," she suddenly blurted out.

"Gordon was murdered, Katherine," he brutally told her. "It was not an accident."

"No, you're wrong Sam." She said, "it was an accident."

"You may want to believe that Kathy but deep down I think you know different."

"No! No! No!" she screamed as she stood and turned her back on him to stare out of the window with her arms folded and tears falling.

"We know the man who did it," he said, "Gordon was on his list along with Penny and Robert Campbell from Stepping Street who he also murdered. You must do the right thing Kathy."

"You mean like you have always done the right thing Sam," she said as she turned and wiped her hardening eyes.

"And what is that supposed to mean?" he asked.

"It means that maybe we do not want you back here sticking your nose in," she said.

"That's harsh Kathy," he said, "I'm only…."

"You're only what, Sam?" she said. "Trying to teach us how to suck eggs."

"Trying to do the right thing," he said, with what was now a defensive tone.

"You mean like waltzing off to London and forgetting we ever existed." she said. "Was that the right thing Sam, was that the right thing?"

"It wasn't like that Kathy and you know it," he answered.

"Well, it sure looks like it to me Sam. There is a guy out there sitting on his bar stool who idolised you and all you can do is come back and throw shit at him. Maybe he is not the full sixpence Sam and maybe he has not always done the right thing but he knows what loyalty means."

"I think emotions are getting the better of you Kathy." he said.

"And of course, you know all about emotions Sam, I wonder how emotional you got about not inviting any of us to your wedding, not even Pete who we all thought would be your best man but of course, all your London cronies were there I suppose"

"That is something I will always regret," he said, "always."

"The best friend anyone could ever wish to have," she said.

"If I could go back I would," he said.

"Well, it's a bit late for that Sam."

"It still does not alter the fact that you were threatened."

"I've told you to forget it."

"Yes, but why were you threatened?"

"Just forget it Sam, please, just forget it."

"Was it over something you know, that I should know?"

"If there was anything, and I told you, maybe they would carry out their threat," she said.

"They might anyway," he told her.

"And maybe they would be doing me a favour."

"For Christ's sake Kathy you can't mean that."

"The trouble with you men," she said, "is that you have no understanding about…"

There was a knock on the door which acted like a ringmaster's bell and allowed them to stop trading punches. Kathy went to it and he heard her whispering to Sally the young barmaid telling her she had done the right thing and not to worry. Before returning to her seat she went to the art-deco glass fronted cocktail cabinet and pulled out a bottle of gin along with a bottle of tonic water and two lead crystal hand cut glasses and placed them on the coffee table in front of them. She then continued to pour herself a drink that consisted of much more gin than tonic before pushing the other glass across to Salt suggesting he could do the same, but he declined.

She broke the silence by telling him that Colly had forgotten his wallet and only had enough on him for a couple of pints so he asked Sally if he could set up a tab, and though it was against the rules of the house she gave her permission.

"So, you allowed it just for him," said Salt.

"I did," said Kathy with a certain amount of satisfaction.

"Can I ask?" he said, choosing his words carefully, "how you came to attain this place?"

"How I came to attain it Sam," she said, while emphasizing his chosen word, "is none of your bloody business."

"Do you rent it or lease it or own it?" he asked, along with a clarity and a calmness that had come back to him about such situations.

"It's all mine," she told him.

"And how did you pay for it?" he asked.

"Again, none of your business Sam," she replied.

"I can always find out Kathy," he said.

"And I cannot understand why you need to know," she said,

"I just need to know Kathy."

"With cash," she reluctantly told him.

"And where did the cash come from?" he asked.

She took a long drink from her glass then swirled its contents before looking into it and downing the rest.

"Well, you know how Gordon was with his wheeling and dealing," she said, "it was just something he built up over the years, you know, for a rainy day and all that."

"A rainy day?" he mocked. "Like enough to buy The Jockey outright."

"Yes," she said.

"And was he dealing drugs Kathy?" he coldly asked.

"Not dealing," she said, "just recreational you know, personal use and all that. At least, that is what I thought."

"Christ almighty, Kathy," he said and stood himself to walk to the window to look out while she poured herself another gin and tonic.

"I did not know Sam," she said to his back, "I swear to God I did not know, there are loads out there now doing a bit of cocaine and smoking the odd spliff and that's how I thought it was with Gordon until looking in the safe one day after he had left it open."

"And what did you find," he asked, turning to face her.

"I found one hundred and twenty-two thousand pounds," she answered.

"In cash?" he asked in an unbelieving tone.

"In cash," she replied. Then watched his shoulders slump and his face contort into a crumpled sadness as a daggered awareness instantly knifed any hopes of keeping treasured friends, whether dead or alive, out of what he saw as an almighty mess.

"You have to tell me everything Kathy," he said, "this thing is out there now and investigations would continue anyway without me trying to keep you out of it."

"I don't want to get you into trouble Sam," she said.

"Maybe it's time I got myself into trouble," he said, then pulled the other glass towards him and poured a long tonic before adding the gin.

"I can't believe you said that," she uttered, along with an impish look that tried to add a touch of humour to the seriousness that had engulfed them.

In return he smiled but knew he had no choice other than to carry on.

"Now I know," he said, "that you cannot walk into an agent's office and dump a load of cash on the desk and ask to buy The Jockey, so how did all that come about."

"It was done through an accountant," she told him.

"And who was the accountant?" he asked.

"It was Robert Campbell," she replied.

"So, they did know each other," he said, almost to himself.

"Yes," she replied.

Salt was rarely shocked. Anticipation was the name of a game he usually played to perfection.

The obvious did not normally escape him but never had he been personally involved in the way that he was involved now. Maybe he had not seen what he should have seen because deep down he did not want to. Maybe psychologically he wanted the can of worms left unopened. Joining the dots had always been his forte but this time round he had not even spotted the dots. Now those dots were looming large and staring him in the face adding even more pieces to a long and complicated puzzle that was far from being completed.

"And how the bloody hell did Robert Campbell pull that one off?" he asked her.

"I don't know," she replied. "All I can tell you is that the pub was up for sale for slightly more than that but he told us that if we gave him the cash, he could swing it our way."

"So, you gave him one hundred and twenty-two thousand pounds in cash and trusted him?"

"Yes," she said.

"You could have lost the lot," he said.

"That's nothing compared to what I have lost Sam," she said, "what does it matter?"

"It matters because you could be in danger," he said,

"They can only put a bullet through my head and that would be a blessing in disguise," she said.

"You cannot mean that Kathy," he said.

"Oh yes I can," she replied.

He wanted to put his arms around her and offer some kind of comfort but knew that his offer would be rejected.

"Anyway," she continued, "after about four months we went into the agent's office with Robert, signed a few papers, and the pub was ours."

There was much more he wanted to ask but knew that now was not the right time and stood to leave. Prior to opening the door, he looked back at her but she did not return his gaze. Stepping into the bar he noticed that Colly was still on his stool but was now chatting to one of the ladies while the other had joined the dominoes team. He then motioned to Sally who was at the other end of the counter and after she came to him asked her what Colly was drinking and would she pour him a pint. Colly had his back to him when he placed the pint under the nose of his old friend who turned expecting to see the face of Kathy doing what she often did. There was a long and awkward silence with the two of them looking deep into each other's eyes before Colly simply said, "Thank you,"

"Enjoy," said Salt, who turned to walk away but noticed that Kathy had come from her room and had witnessed the scene.

"Thank you for that Sam," she said, as he walked past and only paused briefly before exiting her domain.

Outside it was raining cats and dogs as his mother used to say so he pulled his coat collar up for protection but at the same time lifted his face to the heavens to feel the rain upon his face.

*The picture is right for completion
but the piece that is left does not fit.*

Chapter Ten

Homeward Bound

The cats and dogs turned into a deluge as raindrops as big as sixpenny pieces bounced off his car roof and the pavements and the tarmac. He looked on as the drains refused to take the torrents and the road began to flood as it always did. Seeing it now shredded his half a lifetime away into a ghostly nothingness. Surely it was only yesterday when the three of them left the Galleon and waded through the almost knee-deep water daring the outburst to do its worst while others eyed their bravado or stupidity from the shelter of shop doorways. He decided to stay put as the sensible ones did back then, and while waiting for this outburst to abate switched on the radio to be greeted by Paul Simon singing one of his favourite songs and concluded it was not love that lay waiting silently for him but maybe something much more sinister.

There were now new considerations with the overriding one being his commitment. Something he had never contemplated before in all his years in the force. Never had personal involvement clouded assessments that were normally as icy as those bitter cold winter mornings waking up as a boy to the sight of jack frost embellishing the metal framed windows of his tiny bedroom. He even found himself wondering if Mary was right about coming back but latched on to the thought that life had taught him never to let pass by that which was meant to be, A sudden unhealthy urge found him wishing that he still smoked and that Yorke was sitting beside him so that he could cadge one of his Capstan Full Strength. He imagined inhaling deep into his lungs and purposely holding the smoke in before slowly exhaling his doubts and his newly acquired apprehensions.

The rain ceased almost as suddenly as it had started and the sun came out and he knew that emanating from the fields up from the farm would be that lovely sweet petrichor smell his grandfather had first pointed out to him. A smell that had not graced his nostrils for many years.

He was just about to pull away from the kerb when he noticed Kathy waving for his attention from the doorway of The Jockey and stopped and switched off the engine. She was holding her hand up to her ear suggesting a phone call was waiting for him.

"I thought they could contact you in that," she said, nodding towards his car as he walked across.

"A problem waiting to be fixed," he said.

"It's your man Benson," she said, "from the station, he thought he would find you here."

Colly was still sitting at the bar but this time he sat alone and did not turn as Salt entered and was ushered back into Kathy's lounge. She pointed to the phone sitting on the Art-Deco sideboard along with photographs of Gordon and her in happier times.

"Yes, you've lost so much," he said as he laid his hand on the receiver.

"I know," she said as she walked back to the door to allow him his privacy.

"Benson?" said Salt.

"Patrick Mannion has been found hanging in the back room of his shop," said Benson.

"Dead? I presume," said Salt.

"Yes sir," Benson replied.

"When?" Salt asked.

"About twenty minutes ago sir."

"Who found him?"

"Her name is Susan, a shop assistant who has worked for Mannion's for over twenty years."

"And who is there now?"

"I sent Crockett and Edwards and Turner," Benson replied.

"So not yourself?" said Salt.

"I decided I had better remain here to link up," he answered.

"Good thinking?" said Salt, "but why send Turner?"

"Because of Susan sir, she is in shock and deeply traumatised and I thought she might react better talking to a woman."

"Was there anyone else in the shop at the time?"

"No sir."

"And is there another door into this back room?"

"No sir," said Benson, "only the one from the shop."

The essence of shock was rarely applicable to those with policing experience, but to the likes of Salt it was non-existent. Even so his ability to dismiss it completely and immediately fashion his mind to the job in hand never failed to astound and sometimes even frighten Benson by the coldness exhibited.

"No suspicions of foul play then," Salt asked

"It certainly looks like he took his own life," said his sergeant.

"Okay Benson," he said, "I'll make my way over so tell the others to expect me."

"Will do sir."

The bar had now emptied except for Kathy collecting a few glasses from various tables and placing them on the counter ready to be washed and stashed away.

"Did you know Patrick Mannion?" he asked her.

"Of course," said Kathy, "everyone with businesses in the town knew him. Why,"

"Because he has just been found dead," he told her. "Suicide."

"Christ!" said Kathy as she placed two glasses on the bar and leaned against it as if in need of support. "He was only in here last night."

"Did he come in often?" asked Salt.

"Maybe a couple of times a week," she answered, "just popped in for a pint on his way home from work."

"Did he ever associate with Gordon?" he then asked.

"Associate!" she blurted mockingly, "what sort of bloody police speak is that, Sam"

"You know what I mean Kathy," he said.

"No, I do not bloody well know what you mean Sam. Do you mean like Lennon associated with McCartney or Bonnie associated with Clyde or perhaps Judas Iscariot associated with Jesus?"

If he had not been aware before he now realised, he was not interviewing that twenty-year-old from years ago.

"Did they ever do business together?" he asked, ignoring her references.

"And when you say business Sam, what do you mean by business?" she put to him.

"Did they, for instance, ever deal drugs together?" he asked, without sugar-coating his approach.

"I have already told you that I did not know he was dealing drugs until I came across that money so I could not have known if they were dealing, could I? Their only common association as you put it was their Masonic membership"

"Stinky was a Mason?" he unbelievingly blurted out. "How come I never knew?"

"Because you were not here to find out Sam," she coldly told him.

"So, Gordon and Mannion were Masons?" he asked, ignoring the emotional attachment she had brought into the interview.

"Yes." She answered.

"And Robert Campbell who proffered the purchase of this property?"

"Yes, I believe he was also a Mason," she told him.

"And the agent from the property company, whose name I will now need?"

"I do not know Sam, but I do know that you seem to be implying something improper about their membership when from what I read the Yard is inundated with Masons"

"I would not go as far as to say inundated but there are quite a few."

"Including yourself Sam?" she asked "Now can you tell me," he said, without answering her question, "if the name Robin Dalton means anything to you or meant anything to Gordon?"

"It means nothing to me but I cannot answer for Gordon."

"Okay Kathy that is all for now but I shall need to speak to you again," he said in what she thought to be an authoritative voice rather than the voice of a friend.

Stepping out of The Jockey into the spring sunshine with the roads now steaming he spotted a gesticulating Colly spouting what he imagined would be the kind of vocal garbage that still haunted him. The recipient was one of the drinking ladies who seemed to be listening politely as he swayed slightly and shrugged his shoulders while raising his palms and his eyes to the sky with those gestures that are particular to drunken men. Yet when he finished, she put her arms around him and gave him a hug before kissing the side of his cheek and walking away with a small wave of her right hand. As she walked away Colly stepped towards his car with its keys in his hand but was halted from using them as Salt stood between him and the vehicle.

"Give me the keys Colly," he said.

"And why the fuck should I?" asked his friend.

"Because you are not fit to drive," replied Salt, "now hand them over."

"And what will you do if I won't, arrest me?"

"If you get into that car. Yes," said Salt.

"What for Sam, another notch on the belt?"

"No," said Salt, "to save you going to court and perhaps even prison for drunk driving."

"But if you don't arrest me nobody will be any the wiser." Said Colly.

"And what if that wisdom comes from killing some innocent kid or knocking a cyclist off his bike or crashing a red light at the crossroads?" said Salt.

"It hasn't happened yet," came the reply.

"There's always a first time," said Salt, "and then they will throw the book at you. Now give me the keys Colly."

"So, how do you expect me to get back home then, Detective Chief Inspector Salt?"

"I'll take you myself," said Salt, ignoring Collie's sarcastic tone.

The drive back to Stepping Street took place in silence until Salt pulled up outside of the house then with an earnestness that surprised him heard his friend say, "Thank you Sam."

"I just don't want to visit you in prison." Said Salt.

"I mean it Sam," said Colly, "I also needed telling. It will not happen again."

"You mean you are going to give up the demon drink," joked Salt, but Colly ignored the comment and while placing his hand on the back of Salt's which sat on the gearstick said, "We had something special you know Salty, you and I, we had something special."

"We certainly did," said Salt, and although he knew that the melancholia came as much from the booze as it did from the man, he also knew that it came from the heart.

"Now bugger off and get that granddaughter of yours to make you a couple of stiff black coffees, and don't go back for the car until tomorrow." he said.

"She's not in," said Colly.

"Where is she?" asked Salt.

"She started that job," said Colly, and said it as if he thought Salt would know what he was talking about.

"You know, the one that that pretty young constable found for her," he continued.

"I know nothing about it," said Salt.

"Thought she would have told you," Said Colly.

"No," said Salt.

"They met in the town," Colly explained, "and your young copper told her she had heard of a job going at the steel works and thought it would suit her, so she got the interview and started more or less straight away."

"That's brilliant," said Salt, "but what about the child?"

"She pops her into a nursery on the way to work and the kid loves it," said Colly. "She said at first it wasn't worth going but I told her I would pay for the nursery."

"You know he's not such a bad guy," echoed Kathy's words.

"It's none of my business but I've wondered why she lives with you instead of her parents," said Salt.

For a long time Colly did not answer but when he did it came with a sudden sober seriousness that surprised his former friend.

"Drugs," said Colly. "Both of them big time. They are rife around here now Sam, but I did not expect my own daughter to get hooked."

"I'm sorry," said Salt.

"Now I'm not telling you so that you go bursting their door down and...."

"That will not happen Colly," said Salt cutting in. "I promise, that will not happen"

"I caught her once," he went on. "Injecting, and it made me want to throw up. Their house is a tip and poor Gail, who is a good kid Sam, she really is a good kid, has had to harden herself to virtually losing her parents."

"I'm sorry," Salt said again.

"I know I'm not the brightest in the pack Sam and done stuff I am ashamed of, but I've worked bloody hard all my life to provide and this is like a kick in the teeth. I just don't know what to do Sam, I don't know what to do."

Salt sensed him being next to tears and knew his friend would not want those tears to fall in front of him so made excuses about moving on but not before saying that he was always there for him if he wanted to talk.

"I might just do that Chief Inspector," joked Colly "I might just do that."

"Anytime," said Salt.

"You know you are not a bad sort after all," said Colly. then opened the car door and stepped out onto the pavement.

"But I can be a right bastard sometimes," said Salt along with the biggest of smiles which Colly returned as he slammed the door and made his way up to the house.

Watching the slumped shoulders disappear into the tiny terraced building Salt could not help but share the despair he saw entering that house and suddenly realised that his coming back was not just about himself. Compelled as he was to return, he was now questioning that compulsion, and maybe that is how it is when you age, he thought. Maybe this time the cuckoo was wrong and those early adumbrated cloudy images that always trailed a path towards illumination would this time fail to find their way towards the light. Already the guilt complexes and unanswerable questions were kicking in.

"Should he tell Colly about Stinky and his drug dealing?"

"How would that affect the relationship between Kathy and Colly?"

"Was Kathy aware of the daughter's heroin addiction and was Stinky the supplier?"

"If true how would Colly react if he found out?"

Every question now carried the weight of personal involvement and it was a weight he was not sure he wanted to carry. The fact over feeling format rigorously adhered to at the Yard that checked any emotional dimension no longer applied.

Just across the road to his right, the ghost of a beautiful angelic young lady looked down with smiling eyes into the fawning face of an adoring adolescent. To his left, a stuttering Mr Hall with Rachel beside him stood in their doorway silhouetted by a Christmas warmth and placed a sixpence into that adolescent's hand. And that adolescent now realised he was diving into something much deeper than trying solve what might turn out to be the unsolvable.

Home,
where a life lies waiting
silently for me.

Chapter Eleven

By Bread Alone

"If a man has two loaves, he should eat one, and sell the other to buy flowers" was the old Chinese proverb that came to Salt as he approached Mannion's after parking the car and noting that the modern idiom of placing posies had already begun.

Even as he lifted the barrier tape that prohibited entry for the passer-by, the young uniformed bobby who had checked his credentials was handed a bunch of daffodils which he laid down in front of the jewellers, bringing Salt to think that in his time he had not bought enough flowers, and he did not mean the presently abundant Genus Narcissus.

Just before entering he took a long hard look down the high street. A street that once had an array of varied and interesting shops. But now, the butcher, the baker, and the candle stick maker had long gone. Along with chemists and hardware shops and tailors and ladies fashion shops and florists. Woolworths had gone. Millets and Mace had gone. Parkwell's, the town's only high-class furniture shop had gone. Even the thriving market hall with its many stalls had closed.

What he saw saddened him. The shut-up shop fronts with their pulled down metal shutters saddened him even more. Every cinema except The Scala had closed their curtains for the last time. The foyers no longer thronged with a Saturday night expectancy.

The town now had a grimy look whereas once upon a time it gleamed.

He had never had a head for dates. Occurrences came and went and were often recalled with utmost clarity, but ask him to place them in the passage of time and a frown would crease his brow. He was not a chronologist. Even his wedding year had to be worked out although every detail of the day remained photographically locked away.

As was the day when they entered the shop hand in hand to buy the rings. He could still picture the svelteness of the ageing silver haired owner greeting them with the broadest of smiles and remembered him wearing a slate blue mohair suit being way above any cut that he could afford.

He remembered the grandfather clocks softly ticking adding an ambience that eased you into a sense of well-being and recalled the glass cabinets being adorned with vintage pieces lying next to modern designs. The seemingly endless choice of rings and watches and bracelets and necklaces all adorned with diamonds he had never forgotten. But most of all he remembered the smell and an aura that was the same then as it was now. Being obsessed with the present is often an antidote to remembering the past, but this was not so with Salt.

He had never met Patrick Emerald Mannion whose middle name carried a family tradition started years back of another precious offspring inhabiting a very precious planet. Neither had he entered the place since that time of the rings but doing so now he was immediately struck by the fact that little had changed.

Was it only yesterday that they had walked in?

Was it only yesterday that they tried on their rings?

Was it only yesterday that the Mannion of that time had wished them a full and happy married life and made it seem so personal even though he had done the same so many times before?

He purposely went to the photographic roll of honour to look into those piercing eyes of the last member of this local clan and had to agree with Turner about him having the penetrating gaze of one tough cookie. Yes, he shared the long face and bony cheekbones and protruding chin of those who had gone before him but he most certainly did not share their obvious warmth. So why then did this one tough cookie decide to end his precious time upon this precious planet?

While dwelling on a dynasty that had come to an end, he was joined by Yorke who wished him good morning and informed him that the pathologist had arrived.

"Where is he now?" asked Salt.

"In the strong room with Edwards and the body," replied Yorke.

"And does he go by the name of Paul Minton?" inquired Salt.

"He does sir, you know him?"

"Indeed, I do."

"And did you know Patrick?" asked Yorke while pointing to his photograph.

"No," said Salt, "he arrived while we were in London."

"But being born here, I suppose you knew the rest of the family," said Yorke.

"Not exactly," came the reply, "coming from the wrong side of the tracks, the jewellers were way out of my parents league, as they were for most of our neighbours."

"I can't believe that," said Yorke.

"It was a time when folk struggled to find pennies to buy a bag of coal let alone a cluster of diamonds," said Salt.

"And here's me thinking you were born with the proverbial silver spoon," joked Yorke.

"It was hand-me-downs and holes in shoes for us," said Salt. "I remember going up to the big school and my first pair of shorts being made from blackout."

"What's blackout?" asked Yorke.

"It's a material they used during the war to blackout windows." Salt told him.

"So, no fancy trainers and a Man United strip?" said Yorke.

Salt did not answer but fell into a greyness that matched his memories. He could have told this young D.C. so much more but decided his interest would be minimal.

Instead, he pointed to Patrick's predecessor and told him how this quietly-spoken sophisticated man had wished him and Mary a wonderful future.

"The looks have certainly passed down," said Yorke, "but not it seems the personality."

"A rogue gene, maybe, from long ago," suggested Salt.

"You believe that sir?" asked Yorke.

"We are all from people of the past," answered Salt and then suggested they move on to the strong room.

"We still have choices," said Yorke as they walked towards the door.

"Maybe we do and maybe we don't," said Salt.

"I'm not with you there," said Yorke.

"What choice, for instance, did Judas have?" asked Salt.

"I am not religious," said Yorke, along with a puzzled brow.

"Neither am I," stated his boss.

"Then I don't understand your reasoning sir," said Yorke.

"Well, without Judas where would Jesus be?" said Salt, "he had to play his part."

"As in all the worlds a stage and all that crap," joked Yorke.

"You could have hit the nail on the head," said Salt.

Then, being the leading man in their present drama he took it upon himself to enter the strongroom first but hesitated in the doorway to take in the scene. The corpse lay in the middle of the room where it had been pulled to attempt resuscitation. Paul Minton was crouched over the body taking photographs and Edwards was standing against the back wall with his arms folded watching Minton go about his work. Attached to the bars of a small high window still hung the cut off rope and to the right of Edwards lay the fallen kitchen chair which Salt assumed Patrick had kicked away to carry out his final act.

The presence of death did not disturb Salt as much as the moment of passing which both perturbed and fascinated him at the same time. "There are moments when the soul takes wings" wrote one of his favourite writers and here he was wondering if this was true in the case of Patrick, and if so, did it wing towards a destination more prized than the precious one it had left behind?

"Good morning, Samuel," said Minton, along with a cherubic smile that seemed to accentuate his rotundity and place his personality in a circus ring rather than a crime scene.

"Good morning, Paul," said Salt, "long time no see."

"Obviously I knew you were back because of Penny Campbell," said Minton.

"And thank you for your report corroborating my thinking," said Salt.

"I knew you would know," said Minton while nodding at the same time.

"To me it was obvious," said Salt.

"To you but not to everybody," said Milton.

"Any quick thoughts here?" asked Salt.

"Definitely suicide," came the reply.

"There were only the two of them in the shop," chipped in Edwards, "he told her he was coming in for a certain item but when he had not returned after ten minutes, she came to investigate but found the door locked in such a way that the Chubb people were called in and found him."

"And is she to be trusted?" asked Salt.

"If you wanted to choose the most trustworthy person in this town you would choose Susan Pelt," said Minton.

"I would not know, having been away for so long," said Salt.

"You have had quite a homecoming," commented Minton.

"Not what was intended," said Salt, but immediately dismissed any personal talk by asking for the report as soon as possible.

"You haven't changed, Samuel," said Minton, with an edge to his voice that was picked up by the other two detectives.

"And why should I?" asked Salt.

"For your own sake," said Edwards.

"Well thank you for the advice," stated Salt.

"You can't always stay outside of the box you know Samuel, maybe it's time you made the effort to come in," said Minton.

"As you did when you came back," stated Salt.

"As I did," said the pathologist.

"And maybe I would rather remain my own man," said Salt, whose tone had lost any friendliness.

"And what is that implying?" asked a now stern-faced Minton.

"It implies whatever you want it to imply," said Salt.

"You know Samuel, there is a place for you if you want it," said Minton in a quieter tone trying to refloat the friendliness.

"Like there was a place for him?" questioned Salt while gesturing towards the corpse.

"I don't know what you mean," said Minton.

"Oh, I think you do Paul," said Salt. "Maybe he was forced from his place into this and that makes it a kind of murder."

"Well good luck in proving that in a court of law," said Minton.

"There are other courts out there," said Salt.

"From which you will never emerge as a winner," mocked Minton.

"Perhaps not," said Salt, "but how much do I have to lose to become one, Paul?"

The two men looked long and hard at each before Minton slung his camera over his shoulder and exited the strongroom.

With their eyes naturally drawn to the body the three detectives fell into a respectful dignified silence that seemed to emanate as much from the dead Mannion as it did from them. It was Yorke who broke the silence by whispering that he would fetch a blanket to cover the body and at the same time organise the hearse.

"You have history with Minton?" Edwards tentatively asked when they were alone.

"Was it that obvious?" asked Salt

"You could say that," answered Edwards.

"He ended up in London the same as me," Salt told him. "And our paths crossed on several occasions before he came back here,"

"So, you are both local," said Edwards.

"Very much so," said Salt, "but poles apart, we lived up on The Spinney council estate while his family lived in Upper Collaston."

"The posh part," said Edwards.

"The posh part," agreed Salt.

"Is that why he sports a dickie-bow?" asked Edwards.

"Could be," said Salt.

"Did you know him before London?"

"No."

"You met him for the first time while at the Yard?"

"Yes."

"And that was to do with work?"

"You seem like a dog with a bone," said Salt with a smile.

"Just interested sir," said Edwards.

"I found out he went to the school I should have gone to," said Salt, talking as much to the still hanging rope as he was to Edwards.

"And why didn't you go?" he was asked.

"After I told my parents I had passed they told me they could not afford the uniform and books."

"You then went to the local comp I suppose.?"

"No comps then, just secondary moderns," said Salt, "you go and get tarred."

"So, Minton also passed for that school," said Edwards.

"No, but money talks," said Salt, taking his gaze away from the rope, "money talks."

"I saw some of that myself," said Edwards.

"It was rife then," Salt told him. "They somehow got him into Uni as well. Never did his national service while most of us did our two-year stint in the army the navy or the air force,"

"Which service for you?" asked Edwards.

"The army," answered Salt, "they were two years that decimated my naivety."

"Never had to do it myself," said Edwards.

"You missed out big time," said Salt.

"And why did he leave London?" asked Edwards,

"Because of his incompetence," said Salt bluntly.

"So how did he get the job back here," asked Edwards.

"It's not what you know," hinted Salt, but then realised he had probably said too much. Not only about Minton but also about himself. It was not in his make up to be so self-revealing but the awkward air that filled the room brought thoughts he had no intention of expressing. The body could not be ignored. Every time death plays its part, he thought, and upstages us.

Yorke came back with the blanket and placed it thoughtfully over the young man's body before telling Salt that the hearse was on its way and that Turner had asked if she could take the traumatised Susan Pelt home or to hospital.

"I would like a word with her first," said Salt.

The rest room consisted of a small kitchen area with a period sofa on the opposite wall and a dining table in the middle of the room. Around the table were three chairs. Salt guessed that the fourth one was the one Patrick had taken into the strongroom and kicked away. The walls were not only decorated with a William Morriss paper but were also adorned with many etchings and paintings and old photographs of the town. It was probably the finest rest room that Salt had ever seen which he thought spoke volumes about this old-fashioned family firm.

Turner was sitting with Susan on the sofa holding her hand. When he entered, she looked up but Susan did not. Salt guessed that she was most likely well past retirement age. He pulled out one of the chairs and sat opposite her.

"My name is Chief Inspector Salt," he said, "and if you don't mind, Susan, I would like to ask you a few questions about what happened today."

"I know it's not easy," he continued, "but sometimes it is important to…."

"My mother will be coming soon," said Susan before he could finish.

"And where is your mother now?" Salt asked, in the softest tone he could find.

"She's baking cakes," said Susan.

"And where is she baking cakes?" asked salt

"In heaven," replied Susan, "but she's coming soon."

He turned and looked at Turner, who gave a shrug and a and a gentle shake of the head.

"I've never seen anyone that bad," said Salt.

"It's shock," Turner told him. "My sister went like that after our father died."

They were now talking freely and openly in front of her.

"Has she family?" asked Salt.

"I asked Yorke to inquire next door," answered Turner, "and they told him that she has lived alone since her mother died, but had recently taken in a godson to live with her.""

"No other family?"

"Not as they know of," replied Turner, "they said her life revolved around the shop and the church where she played the organ. They did mention a friend called Audrey Kirke who also attended St Cuthberts but did not know how to contact her."

"Did you say Audrey Kirke?" asked Salt.

"Yes sir, do you know her?"

"I most certainly do. Now let's organise that ambulance and get her into hospital."

"If you don't mind, I would like to take her myself," said Turner.

"Then you do that," said Salt.

"Thank you, sir," she replied.

"No. Thank you," said her boss, "and thank you for organising that job for Gail Shepherd."

"How did you find out?"

"Her grandfather told me."

"She's a good kid you know sir, who's had it tough. Deep down, she is a good kid."

"And so are you Turner," he said, just before he stepped back into the shop to witness Patrick vacating his business for the last time.

After telling Yorke and Edwards to secure the premises he walked out of the shop to be greeted by a misty thin soundless rain. Night was falling. The high street was now deserted. The metal shutters replaced the well-lit windows he so vividly remembered, bringing a sadness shared by so many of his generation. The street lamps seemed to accentuate an obvious dowdiness that had replaced the warmth and vibrancy of yesterday. He pulled his coat collar up at the back and brought his lapels together at the front with his left hand, then asked the young constable his name and how long he had been standing there.

"It's Baker sir, and I've been here about four hours," came the reply.

"And how long have you been in the force?"

"Two years sir."

"You like it?"

"I love it."

"And are you local, Baker?"

"From The Spinney sir, if you know it."

"I know it well," said Salt. "Now can you tell me if there were any whispers going round about Patrick Mannion?"

The constable hesitated before telling Salt that there were whispers but nothing proved.

"About what?"

"About drugs sir. My opinion was that he was involved in some way."

"Dealing?" asked Salt.

"Possibly sir, but word on the estate was that he was being protected."

"Who by?"

"Don't know sir."

"Well can I ask you to keep your ears open Baker."

"Will do sir," came the reply, "but when they know you are a copper, they…"

He was interrupted by a man of about thirty carrying a single carnation asking if he could lay the flower himself. Baker looked at Salt who nodded and the young constable lifted the tape. After laying the carnation the man stood for a few seconds with his head bowed before turning to walk away with tears streaming down his face.

The blooms we stop
to smell today
are fragranced from
a world away.

Chapter Twelve

Skin Deep

It was his birthday, and as was their custom on each other's birthday, they sat at the dining table in dressing gown and slippers enjoying breakfast and opening cards.

"They get less every year," Sam said.

"This is no good for us you know," she said, as bacon and sausage and eggs and baked beans and hash browns were devoured.

"I don't think that twice a year will do us any harm Mary," he replied.

"I don't suppose it will," she said.

"Anyway, how do we stop?" he asked.

"We just stop," she answered.

"So, I don't have to do this in two months' time," he said.

"You most certainly do," she said.

"So, how do we stop?" he repeated.

"I don't suppose we do," she said.

"Unlike my birthday kiss," he said teasingly.

"Sorry," she said and leaned across and pecked him on the cheek and again wished him happy birthday.

"Not the long luscious lingering one then," he said.

"Maybe that will come tonight," she answered.

"I should be so lucky," he said with the broadest of smiles.

"Maybe you will be Samuel Salt," she said, "maybe you will be."

Now it was his turn to reach across with a kiss and a squeeze of her hand before looking at his watch and telling her he would have to get ready to go.

"I have a job," she said before he could rise and walk away.

"A job?"

"Yes," she answered, "volunteering at the hospice shop in the town."

"That's great," he said, "but why didn't you tell me last night."

"Because you were late," she replied, "and not exactly in listening mode."

"Things on my mind." he said.

"There is always something on your mind Sam, perhaps it's time you made it so you did not have things on your mind."

"How do you mean?" he asked.

"You know exactly what I mean," she replied,

"Loads keep working at my age," he said defensively.

"Yes, but they come home and leave their jobs at the office or the factory or the building site."

"I think that's exaggerating Mary,"

"It's not Sam, you come home but you're not home."

"So, you want me to sit here all day twiddling my thumbs."

"You also know that is not what I mean. You have so much to give in other ways Sam, and we could also travel more, even get over to Brisbane to stay with Derek and Joan."

"They were only here last year." he said.

"Yes, and what did he say before they left. Pack it in Sammy boy and come on over."

"I really have to get ready," he said.

"Now don't be late back," she said, "the table is booked for seven."

"I won't," came his reply.

She was still in her dressing gown standing in the doorway with her arms folded as she watched him back the car out into the road ready to drive off.

"There's no reversing time, Samuel Salt," she said to herself as he waved before pulling away.

He had never expected the nostalgia bug to bite, but it had. He had never intended to turn into the sprawling council estate that was part of the post war building boom, but he did. Maybe it was talking to Baker that had brought it on. Maybe it was the need to be part again of what used to be. Mindfully he realised that over the years he had done the estate a disservice. He had forgotten about the open spaces and the green verges bordering most streets. He remembered that they were good houses with bathrooms and downstairs toilets which were luxuries for those coming from back-to-backs sharing an outside privy and only having a bath on Saturday nights with hot water brought from the brew house and tipped into the tin bath.

He recalled playing cricket on the green with Colly and Stinky along with Arnie and Slater and Alfie Jones with a bat made by Colly's dad from a bit of old floorboard and a battered old Castro oil can for wickets. He remembered Georgie (who was as good as any boy) joining in and knocking more sixes than any of them. He had not been here, he thought, when Colly and Stinky moved on, but what about the others, did they still live on the estate? If he had kept in touch he would have known. It occurred to him that Kathy was right and that none of the others would share his wistfulness. The regrets kept building. If he had come to lay ghosts he had failed. The phantoms were too many. Memory lane was not what he thought it would be.

Neither were the houses. Most had been purchased from the council and modernised to such a degree that the estate he had known was not the estate he was experiencing now. Unlike the town it had become a place to be proud of. The saplings that had been planted on the verges all those years ago now towered above the houses giving the estate a welcoming rural feel. Double glazing had replaced the old metal framed windows and front gardens had been turned into drives to park the many cars that were non-existent when he was a boy. No one had a car back then, everyone lived at the same level, now, he saw the latest reg parked next to an old banger.

Pulling up and parking outside of their old house he had forgotten how high it stood up off the road and the many steps the black faced coalmen had to negotiate while humping their heavy-laden sacks. Looking back now he realised how those well-built houses possessed a better spec than many of the private ones of a similar size being built at that time. He remembered his forever aproned mother standing at the Belfast sink and how he would creep up behind her and tie her apron strings into knots. He remembered his father standing at the bottom of those steps with one of his drinking buddies putting the world to rights as only drunken men can. He remembered Sunday School and eventually saying no to it and how the wrath of God never descended, leaving him free to be his own person.

But the reminiscing stopped when he saw the front door to the house open and a tall elegant Tagore lookalike sporting the same kind of beard and length of hair and handsome face descend the steps and make his way towards the car. He wound down the window as the man came nearer and wished him good morning.

"Excuse me sir," said the man without returning Salt's greeting, "but I have observed you looking up at my house for the last five minutes or so and due to recent troubles, I wonder if I should be calling the police."

Their eyes locked and Salt immediately took a liking to the eyes he was looking into.

"I am, a policeman," he said as he removed himself from the car and took his warrant card from his inside pocket and handed it to the man who studied it carefully before handing it back.

"So, Detective Chief Inspector Salt," the man asked, "can I ask you why you are here?"

"I am not here as a copper," Salt replied, "and I am sorry if I have alarmed you, but I am here as someone who lived in that house from the age of about two until leaving in my early twenties, it is the house of my upbringing."

"Is that really true?" asked the man.

"It is true," replied Salt.

"Then you must come in and have tea and see the house as it is now."

"That is very kind of you," said Salt, "but I am already running late. Maybe another time."

"You would be most welcome."

"Do you mind if I ask your name?" inquired Salt.

"And is that Inspector Salt posing the question?" asked the man.

"No," came the reply, "it is Samuel Salt asking."

"Then my name is Kabir."

"Now please excuse my ignorance," said Salt, "but is that your first name or you surname?"

"It is my first," the man answered, "my name is Kabir Chandra."

"It has been a pleasure to meet you Kabir," said Salt and held out his hand.

"The same applies," said Kabir as the two shook hands, "please you make sure you come back."

"I will," said Salt as they locked eyes again and knew that they liked each other. "Now before I go can you tell me what trouble you have been experiencing."

"I think you know," said Kabir.

"I'm sorry," said Salt.

"It happens," replied Kabir, "it happens in my own country and it happens here."

"You speak like a pragmatist," said Salt.

"Just a realist," said Kabir while shrugging his shoulders.

"You know, you remind me of a certain writer," Salt told him just before getting into the car.

"And you remind me of a certain film character," said Kabir. "Except your skin is the wrong colour."

"Now I'm not with you there," said Salt, with a perplexed look.

"And you're supposed to be the detective," said Kabir.

"Looks like I will have to have a clue," said Salt.

"Well, maybe it will come to you in the heat of the night," said Kabir.

Then, with a slight bow of the head, turned, and made his way back up the steps to the house.

Salt was about a mile away before the proverbial penny dropped and the biggest of smiles came across his face.

****

His decision to be first in The Blue Room for the next meeting was as much a decision for seeking solitary reflection and a prepared mind as it was for the need to be ahead of the others.

And his view of the three leafless sycamores aided his need like nothing else in the world. The riverine landscapes of the Thames brought their rewards but this was home. This was the omphalos of his being. This was the centre of his mindful universe. He might have left it, but it had never left him. Even the scattered sheep looking like little white boulders on the green slopes down from the hedgerow added a natural solace that had been so difficult to find in the capital.

Beyond the hedgerow lay Sixteen Acres and memories of partridges scaring the living daylights out of them as they suddenly rose up from the stubbled corn. Following on came the field where he could still visualise his mother and grandmother kneeling in the bitter cold, docking beet with hessian sacks as aprons. Down from there was the coppice where his grandad and his uncles would take the tractor and flush the rabbits from their burrows before shooting what they needed. There was always a rabbit hanging behind the cellar door on the farm, but all that stopped when myxomatosis was introduced, with some welcoming the introduction while others stated that the authorities had killed off the working man's meal.

Turner entered first and broke his concentration. He turned and smiled and inquired about Susan Pelt.

"I've just come from seeing her on the ward and she is back to normal and ready to be discharged," said Turner.

"I have never seen anyone go like that before," said Salt.

"Apparently it is not the first time." Turner told him.

"Says who?"

"Says Audrey Kirke sir," answered Turner, "who assured me that Susan will be looked after. She also inquired after you sir"

"If Audrey Kirke says she will be looked after then you should have no qualms," said Salt.

"She seemed a very formidable lady if you don't mind me saying," said Turner.

"An outspoken force to be reckoned with Turner," he said, "but a force for the good things of this world which she wants to bring to everyone she meets or at least open their minds to."

"She emits a kind of likeable arrogance," noted Turner.

"I could not have described her better myself," said Salt, "but believe me it is an arrogance that is cultured towards the well-being of others, even if they do not know it."

"So, both coming from the same town you knew her before you went to London." She asked.

"Not at all," replied Salt, "I had been there some fifteen years or so and my name had appeared in the papers on a couple of occasions regarding certain cases when she wrote and asked if I would give a talk at their next Leprosy Mission meeting at St Cuthberts."

"Why you, for that?" asked the young detective.

"I asked her the same question," said Salt.

"And what was her answer?"

"She answered by saying that not all afflictions are obvious to the eye and with that in mind she was sure I would come up with worthwhile talk as their guest speaker."

"And did you?"

"I like to think so."

"That's twice that's come up sir," she said.

"I'm not with you," said her boss.

"Leprosy, sir," said Turner, "Benson talked of lepers looking through the window at Culbone."

"Then there has to be a third time," said Salt.

"And you believe that sir?" she asked.

"No but my mother did," said her boss, and then seemed to edge into a reflectiveness that saw him talking as much to himself as to her.

"After finishing my talk Audrey came up to me and in no uncertain terms told me not to leave the country in the next couple of weeks and when I told her we were booked to fly to the U.S two weeks from that date she told me to cancel."

"And did you?"

"No," said Salt, "but on the day before flying I became nauseous and started vomiting and my skin started tightening around my body to make me feel I was being crushed into nothingness and I started slurring my words and the next thing I know is that I am waking up in hospital."

"And what was it?" asked Turner.

"Severe septic shock," said Salt, "they put me into an induced coma. It was three days before I came round with the consultant telling me that if I had boarded, I would have left that plane in a body bag."

"How do you think she knew?"

"When she came to visit me, I asked her and she just said. "We are all deeper than our skin Samuel. We are all deeper than our skin.""

"I don't understand,"

"Neither did I,"

"And that was it?"

"Well, no, not quite," he said, "when I pushed for more, she said that there are laws other than those that I represent."

"Meaning?" asked Turner.

"Meaning," answered Salt, "That Audrey Kirke is a law unto herself."

"They seem to be on the same level," she whispered while looking past Salt to also take in the framed idyllic scene.

"I'm not with you," said Salt.

"My uncle," she said, "and your friend Audrey, they seem to exist on the same plane."

It was obvious to him that the story had fascinated her and she was about to pursue it further when Edwards walked in followed by the others.

He watched them settle and was pleased with his crew. Pleased that he could mix and match as he had done at the Yard. Pairing was important for corroboration and confidence. The testimonies of a trusted two are difficult to break down whereas a single officer without the confident backing of a colleague can sometimes find the twisting barrage of a bruising barrister quite daunting. Many times, he had seen young officers belittled by such barrages when all they were doing was speaking the truth, the whole truth, and nothing but the truth.

Even the new boys had slotted in nicely he thought, as he observed Best walking in chatting to Crocket and Briggs while sharing some kind of joke.

On his way to the board, he picked up Benson's headmaster's cane and remembered old man Green starting to give him six of the best in the woodwork class for some triviality, and how every stroke became more vicious than the one before because of his contumacious refusal to wince or show any kind of discomfort. He recalled defiantly staring into his teacher's eyes daring him to do his worst and the teacher responding with a seemingly sadistic approach to the punishment. The third stroke came from as high as the cane could be taken and lashed his palm with such force that the stick snapped.

"You can now return to your bench, Salt," said the teacher when he had finished. "With a lesson learnt I hope."

"But not the one you think you have given, Sir" came the rebellious reply.

"We have five fatalities connected to this case," he stated from in front of the board with that bard-like boom that would not have disgraced certain soliloquies. "We have three murders, one suicide and an accident."

"Penny Campbell," he continued while pointing to her photograph, "had her neck snapped in her own home by a professional killer who called himself Ulrich. The same man who murdered her husband Robert and Gordon Talbot who was landlord at The Jockey. We know this because of a diary that was found after his own fatal accident. How he brought about Campbell's apparent heart attack and staged Talbot's car crash we do not know but bring them about he most certainly did, and then we have young Mannion hanging himself. Why?"

"We have the murdered and the murderer," chipped in Edwards.

"But not the paymaster," said Salt, "who is as guilty as the assassin himself. We are looking for connections and motives. We are looking for anything to tie them all together. It is already known that Talbot was dealing drugs but who was supplying him? We are aware that Robert Campbell assisted Talbot's widow in using drugs money to purchase The Jockey. Why would a highly respected accountant with an international company take such a risk? Is that company involved? After all it is based in Dresden and Ulrich apparently came from that city."

"Even him being murdered shows he was implicated," said Crockett.

"Absolutely," said Salt. "What we do not know is if Campbell and Talbot colluded beforehand but I believe they did."

"Do you think Talbot was aware that Campbell was murdered or even aware that he was targeted before the actual killing or implicitly involved himself?" asked Yorke.

Salt thought long and hard before answering. He even turned and walked to the window to stare out and take in a thought that had not occurred to him and should have done. Was his old friend capable of such machinations he asked himself and then returned to the board.

"My answer is that I do not know," he told them, "Most of you are aware of my old friendship with him and my initial thought was that the friend I knew was not capable of such deeds."

"The connection is cocaine," said Briggs interrupting, "it is fast becoming socially acceptable with almost everyone knowing someone who dabbles. Not many towns in the country are unaffected and yours is now suffering from the leniency of this acceptability. It is possible your pal thought he was doing people a favour which is what the big boys love. Cocaine leads to heroin and that is a totally different ball game. I also must ask if his wife knew or was even complicit in his dealing?"

Because of his experiences Salt fully understood Brigg's explanation of the burgeoning narcotics industry spreading its vile tentacles into every aspect of a society that was both unprepared and ignorant of the evil involved. He remembered the naïve unawareness of his early teenage years and picking up a book from Millets and Mace called The Man with the Golden Arm and being horrified that such a world not only existed but could possibly export itself from the States to our shores. And so, it had. Over the years.

"If Kate Talbot is guilty of anything untoward, we will throw the book at her," he said, while looking directly at Briggs.

"I hope you do not think there was any implication in my asking, sir," said Briggs.

"You were just doing your job," replied Salt, "I would not expect anything different."

"I've been wondering why Patrick Mannion was not targeted in the way that the other two were," said Turner, while throwing another thought into the ring. "After all we know for sure that he was involved in some way. He was a regular at The Jockey meeting up with Talbot which I know proves nothing but we also know he kept the rendezvous at Culbone meant for Campbell and maybe even his wife. Was he meant to be there anyway or did he turn up instead after the accountant was murdered. With the diary being locked up in the Devon house he must have had prior knowledge. Was the diary a target for Ulrich who most surely would have attained it had it not been for the vigilance of Byschov? Who was the mystery man he met up with at that remote place and what was in the package that was exchanged?"

"That leaves quite a few avenues to explore," said Salt.

"Another thought, is that he did not come back to me with records of the Campbell's purchases," continued Turner.

"The drugs world is awash with cash," said Briggs, "not much of it is banked, so I am surprised that Campbell banked his."

"He did not bank all of it," said Benson, "we have yet to find out how the Devon house was purchased but we do know he spent a small fortune renovating it, all paid for in cash."

"Most of it is very cleverly laundered," said the bespectacled Best, "so I too am surprised that a man of his standing and knowledge splashed it the way that he did."

"Sometimes money changes people," piped in Yorke, "they become cocky and arrogant and armoured in an attitude that blinds them to the thought that such an armour can be pierced."

"I think we have taken it as far as we can today," said Salt. "We have new paths and new ideas to explore, but I think we can be sure that these crimes are connected to the impact of the drugs world and all its destructive elements being deeply entrenched in our town. It also seems, and I stress the word seems, because I do not want things taken for granted until proved, that Campbell and Talbot and Mannion were heavily involved, but who is the kingpin who organised three executions and probably forced Mannion into hanging himself. Which makes it a kind of murder also. Is that a local or someone from further afield?"

"There is just one more person I would like to add to the equation, sir," said Turner, knowing that he would be aware of what she was going to say and had already warned her not to.

"And that person is Robin Dalton, who is the brother of Mrs Campbell and her sister. He lives with the sister up at Mill House and when we interviewed them there was something about him that just did not add up," she said, while looking across at her boss who she expected to be glaring angrily at her but found him staring at the floor.

"And can we ask what that something is?" asked an almost sniggering Crocket.

It has already started thought Salt, if she does not take care, she will be bloody crucified and her career could end here and now.

"I just had this feeling that…"

"So now that something turned into feelings," said Crocket along with a smug satisfactory smile.

And here is me thinking she had been totally accepted thought Salt, but it is still there lurking below the surface, not only is she a woman she is also…

"I had this feeling," she repeated defiantly, "that the alibi was just too pat and found that not only did he give a speech that night, which he had never done before, he also had too much to drink and upset a few people who obviously and conveniently remembered."

"Maybe this something gave him this feeling about getting pissed and making speeches," said Crocket, who now appeared to be enjoying himself.

"But you know there may just be substance in what she is sensing," said Briggs while pushing his glasses up on to the bridge of his nose. "Certain people at M.K.P.T have been under our radar for quite a while and that includes Dalton." he told them.

Salt darted a glance at Turner and although she was aware she did not return his look but picked up her papers and slowly and deliberately left the room. He was pleased that Briggs had justified her stance on Dalton and knew she would understand why he had not backed her.

> *Honied or olive*
> *or black brown or white*
> *are meaningless words*
> *to the ones without sight.*

Chapter Thirteen
Softlier than Snow

"It was a good meal," said Mary, as they tucked in to just tea and toast on the morning after his birthday treat.

"Mmmm," he replied while immersed in his half of the local paper.

"Well, that's fifty-eight years you won't see again."

"Mmmm."

"Am I talking to the wall?" she asked, but this time got no reply as he turned the page.

"Yes, I'm talking to the wall," she said and returned to her half of the paper.

"Bloody hell," he suddenly blurted out.

"What is it?"

"Dickie Darting," he replied.

"What about Dickie Darting?" she asked.

"He's dead," came Salt's reply as he pointed to the obituary page.

"And am I supposed to know Dickie Darting?"

"I've told you before I worked for him just after leaving school."

"Oh yes I remember now."

"Bloody hell," he repeated, along with a faraway look and a smile.

"Not exactly a normal reaction to someone's death notice," she said as she read for herself after he handed the page across.

"There was nothing normal about Dickie Darting and besides he was ninety-six," said Salt.

"I didn't know he had received an honour," she said, pointing to the page.

"He didn't."

"But it says here Richard. F. Darting. MBE."

"Master Builder Extraordinaire," said Salt, this time with an even bigger smile, "M.B.E."

"And he got away with it?" she asked after eventually cottoning on.

"As far as I know," said Salt.

"And as far as I remember you liked him"

"You could not help but like Dickie Dartford," he said.

"But why did you decide to enter the building trade?"

"I didn't, it was decided for me."

"By whom?"

"The youth employment officer."

"I don't understand."

"After I told him I would like to be a cub reporter he said I could not do that."

"Why not."

"Because that is only for grammar school boys he said and then handed me Dickie Dartford's business card."

"You've never told me that before," she said.

He shrugged his shoulders.

She gave him a quizzical look and shook her head.

"What?" he asked.

"You," she replied.

"What about me?"

"Keeping the world out."

"I don't know what you mean."

"Oh, I think you do Samuel," she said, "I think you do."

He poured himself another cup of tea but she put her hand across her cup as he went to pour one for her also.

"So, how come you became a copper?" she asked, breaking an awkward silence.

"Fate," he replied, "the same as I was fated to work for Dickie Dartford."

His mother had already made sure he was looking smart for his interview but still adjusted his tie before seeing him out of the house and watching him descend the steps while wondering what the world had in store for him.

He found the offices in the same street as The Galleon and opened the door and walked in. A lady about as old as his mother sat behind a mahogany desk typing away on a very large black typewriter but stopped as soon as he entered to look across at him over her half glasses sitting on the end of her nose.

"You must be young Mr Salt," she said.

He had never been called Mister before.

"Yes," he replied.

"Come for your job interview."

"Yes."

"And are you nervous?"

"No," he surprisingly found himself saying.

"Take a seat," she said, and pointed to the only other chair in the room opposite her desk.

"My name is Marion," she continued, then went on to tell him to always go to her with any problems.

"Mr Dartford may own the company," she said, "but I'm really the boss around here,"

He took note of her cheeky smile and decided that he liked her. Looking around he noted the many black and white photographs adorning the walls of building sites in various stages of construction but was particularly drawn to an oil painting of a tall masted yacht over the door of his office. She noticed his interest.

"He originates from Plymouth," she told him. "Have you ever been?"

"I've never even seen the sea," he told her.

"Hence the middle name Francis," she said, thinking he would pick up on it but he did not.

"Is that his yacht?" he asked while looking up at the painting.

"It was," she answered, "many years ago."

"But not now."

"No, just a smaller craft for when he goes back."

"And is that often?"

"About once a month."

"I see."

"And I see you have just gone fifteen," she said while looking down at a piece of paper which he assumed contained his details.

"Yes," came the reply.

"Have you not thought of going on to further education?" she asked.

"I just want a job," he said.

"My son is the same age," she told him." And we have encouraged him to…."

"I just want a job," he cut in.

"I was only trying to…"

"I just want a job," he repeated, not wanting to discuss his personal thoughts.

"I will see if he is ready for you," she said, and with a glaring look, rose from her desk to make her way towards the door beneath the painting and opened it. After a brief consultation she gestured with her right hand for him to enter.

Often in later life he would recall that moment. Aghast at the thought of himself standing in the doorway for what seemed an eternity with a dropped jaw and gaping mouth as he observed the replicated Captain's quarters of an old sailing ship. While he sought the middle of the room Marion exited and closed the door behind him.

He stood transfixed. As he had been only weeks before by a certain poem. As he would be by the silence of a hushed cathedral or the sheer spirituality found in The Michael Chapel on Iona or the tiny oratory at Gaugane Barra. He did not know why, but he was.

Dartford observed the boy observing and noted how he seemed to take in everything around him. He watched him as he ran his hand over the oak panelled walls while looking up at the oak ceiling with a cut glass chandelier hanging from it. The ceiling curved down to a radius window that should have had a blue sky and rising waves fronting it. His future boss watched him as he picked up the sextant on his desk and brushed his fingers over the goose feathered quill as if he were not there Then move over to the green leather topped table to inspect the ancient charts and telescope and an intriguing armillary sphere that sat upon it. It was not until he saw the smile on the boy's face when he peered into the tall birdcage housing a stuffed parrot that he spoke.

"You like what you see young man?" he asked.

But Salt just stood shaking his head as if he could not believe what he was seeing or feeling.

"Someone has left their soul in this room," he found himself saying with no idea where such words came from.

"What makes you say that?" said his future boss.

"I don't know it's just that…."

"Just what?"

"It's just that," then he paused before saying, "there is magic here."

Dartford eyed him long and hard before deciding that upon those slender shoulders that carried an extremely handsome young face sat a wisdom, as yet, unleashed.

"Did you create it yourself?" Salt asked while looking for the first time into eyes that never held anything but a benevolent smile.

"No."

"Then who?"

"His name is Harvey."

"Harvey?"

"Yes, he works for me. In fact, he is my right-hand man."

"A carpenter I presume," said Salt.

"No," came the reply along with the broadest of grins added to his ever-sparkling eyes. "He is a master carpenter."

"How long did it take him?"

"Two years, on and off," he told Salt.

But what he did not tell him which was discovered later through others was that Harvey, like Mr Hall's son, had returned from the war a broken young man weighing only five and a half stone but was given his job back on full pay and was allowed as long as it took to get back to something like normal and that the cabin was part of that healing process.

As Salt took his seat, he was aware of Dartford putting his hand down to his right and hearing a click before the sound of crashing waves filled the room along with the squawking of gulls and the creaking of timbers and a distant voice shouting "Splice the main brace Mr Gordon, splice the main brace."

Then came the music, and although memory never determined whether it came from the deeper husky tones of a violin or the haunting harmonics of a cello it was remembered as orchestrating perfectly with the cutting of the prow through the water and the thought of a distant gull on the wing.

"So, you want to enter the construction industry?"

"Yes," he lied.

"In what form?"

"I don't understand."

"Carpenter? Plumber? Bricklayer?" said the eyes that never left his along with arms that were extended towards him with opened palms facing the ceiling.

"I'm not sure."

"Mmmm."

"So, I have a choice?"

"You do."

"What do you suggest?"

"What I suggest is that you work with different trades for twelve months and at sixteen I will set you up with an apprenticeship of your choice."

"That sounds good."

"It is what I always suggest, it gives a boy a good grounding."

"I'll go for that."

"Good, now when can you start?"

"I leave a fortnight on Thursday."

"You can start on the following Monday?"

"Yes."

"That's it then, the job is yours."

"Thank you, sir,"

"You are going to be late Samuel," she said while carrying crockery to the side of the sink.

"Crikey," he said, looking at his watch, "I was miles away"

"What's new?" she asked.

He sat quietly looking down at the paper but not reading then said. "You know Mary, I hope I have been good for you."

She stopped her washing up but kept her hands in the bowl as she looked out of the kitchen window to see a robin and a blue tit land at the same time on the edge of the bird bath.

"What's brought that on," she asked without turning round.

"Just thinking."

"Thinking what."

"Something Kathy said."

"What did she say."

"She just said, I wonder if Mary wanted to come back."

"And what did you say?"

There was a long pause before he answered.

"I told her that I hadn't asked you."

Only the robin entered the water and dipped his head and splashed his wings before flying off.

"Well, that's true," she said.

"I'm sorry," he told her.

"What for?"

"Because it has only been about me and my career."

"But that's the world we were brought up in Sam."

"I know, but."

"But what?"

"Well, you could have……"

"Could have what?" she cut in, then turned and faced him but not before noticing the most amazing spiders web on the cypress hedge just to the right of the bird bath.

"Perhaps had a career of your own."

"It is what it is Sam," she said. while drying her hands and sitting opposite him. "Anyway, I was happy in London there was always stuff going on."

"Maybe you and Kathy could…." but did not finish as he looked up and saw her shaking her head.

"I will be ok when I start at the shop," she said.

"I'm glad that cropped up for you,"

"Fate," she said, with a smile, "now bugger off and let me get on with my work."

Although still affected by the nostalgia bug he bypassed the estate but thought of his old home most probably being filled with Indian artifacts and furniture and various Gods and knew that his father would not have approved. In the same way that he disapproved of him taking an interest in the Gita or the Upanishads or Sri Ramakrishna.

The mental blocks his father built or had built for him never allowed the foresight needed to climb the ladder and look over. He remembered

Mr Bastion moving in just two doors away and how his father hated him because his political affiliations differed from his own. He never passed the time of day with the man, or clinked glasses with him, but hated him just the same.

The quietness of his mother, he now knew, was a part of him. Her mystique also belonged to him. Her ghost was more influential now than it had ever been.

Yes, he must come back and talk to Kabir for he knew he had found someone sharing the same plane. Someone who had seen the unseen and known the unknown.

He parked in his allotted place and sat for a few moments watching the comings and goings. He watched others arriving for their day not knowing what faced them. He saw squad cars racing out of the gates with sirens blaring.

He eyed a portly Renshaw heading for the station steps still in uniform and remembered how they had both started on the same day. One from college and the other from the school of hard knocks provided initially by Dickie Dartford. Renshaw, he thought, still plodding the same beat towards his pension. Then, reprimanded himself for his cynicism against an officer who probably had an exemplary record for serving a community he had deserted.

Turner and Crockett arrived at about the same time and parked next to each other. After leaving their cars there seemed to be some kind of altercation with Crocket pointing and gesticulating while Turner remained calm. He looked on as Crockett put his face up to hers before walking away only for Turner to call him back and offer her hand which he reluctantly accepted. A gesture, he thought, that was as calculating as any lie had ever seen. Crockett may have won the battle he surmised, but has most certainly lost the war.

It started to snow, and within seconds the flurry turned into a thick fall descending with the kind of silence that only snow can bring. In no time at all the car park and the cars and distant rooftops and trees were white all over. He remembered waking with the knowledge that it had snowed even before he had looked out. He would tell his mother who would not believe him.

But he knew that there was no other silence like it in the world. A silence that could penetrate bedroom walls and frosted metal frame windows and speak as loud as any uttered words. There was a heaviness to it that was as heavy as this present fall.

145

So I come and go
softlier than snow.
Mary Webb.

Chapter Fourteen

The Dreamers of the Day

There was a completeness about snow scenes that almost moved Turner to tears but she did not know why. She watched as others were drawn to the window first before walking to their desks and it soon became obvious that not everyone thought the same.

"I hate the bloody stuff," said Edwards as he settled and started opening folders.

"It's alright on Christmas cards," said Yorke.

"They don't have to drive after gangsters on Christmas cards," said Briggs chuckling to himself.

"Well, I like it," she said and returned to the window again to look out.

What she could not see was Best nodding towards her and pointing to his temple which brought gentle laughter from the others.

She turned knowing that she was the butt of some joke and eyed the faces of each one before focusing on Crockett who opened his palms to the air and shrugged his shoulders and shook his head. After the others also did the same, she raised her two fingers to them before taking her seat to a faint ripple of applause, along with the realisation that there was now a level of acceptance she had not expected. Maybe it started with the arrival Briggs and Best, she thought.

She was still grateful for the backing of Briggs but was still wondering if her boss would have stepped in if Briggs had not.

The despondency displayed by Salt sitting at his desk in his office watching the flakes descend disturbed him deeply. Just when he felt he was in most need of it his natural ebullience had deserted him. Wanting desperately to deliver because of his personal involvement weighed heavily. But it was that personal involvement which brought about such doubts. Maybe he should hand over, he thought. Maybe independent eyes would see the whole scenario in a different light. Maybe emotions were blurring his vision.

The flakes were now fluffily falling like cotton wool balls and falling so slowly that it was possible to pick out one and watch its slow silent descent towards the ground. In no time at all every building was covered giving the town a oneness that was not easy to ignore. Only the distant steeple pointed to a world beyond.

The phone rang but it was a long time before he answered.

"Samuel," said an assured authoritative voice, "I need to speak with you."

"And who am I speaking to?"

"You know very well," answered Audrey Kirke.

"Yes, Audrey," he said, after a long pause and a smile he knew she would be envisaging.

"It's about Susan Pelt," she said.

"What about Susan Pelt?"

"Her godson."

"What about her godson?"

"He's on drugs."

"And what do you expect me to do?"

"I expect you to investigate," she told him.

"I can't go out and investigate everyone in the town on drugs."

"I'm not asking you to investigate everyone."

"So, what is special about Susan Pelt's godson?"

"He is only fifteen," answered Audrey.

Salt dropped his smile and for a few seconds fell as silent as that single snowflake until she asked if he was still there.

"Would you know what he is taking?"

"Cocaine," she told him.

"How the bloody hell can a kid of fifteen afford cocaine?" he asked, while thinking of a lad of a similar age taking on a paper round to pay for his tobacco addiction.

"No need to swear Samuel."

"Sorry."

"It was given to him," said Audrey.

"Nobody gives cocaine," said Salt.

"Patrick Mannion did," she told him.

He went silent again, but this time she waited for him to come back to her.

"And why would he do that?"

"Why do you think.?"

"Christ!" said Salt understanding her insinuation.

"I don't think it actually went that far," said Audrey ignoring his blasphemy, "but I do not think his intentions were exactly honourable."

"Is that what Susan thinks?"

"No, she is too naïve and thinks in a perverse kind of way he was helping Greg by him not having to pay for his habit."

"Is that the lad's name?"

"Yes."

"What do you think?" he asked.

"With his reputation I think it was obvious."

"I didn't know about his reputation."

"Well, you haven't been here to find out have you," she said, in a flat matter of fact tone.

"That's true," he said, "but one of my officers did think he leaned towards…."

"Well, she was absolutely right," cut in Audrey.

"I didn't say the officer was female," said Salt.

"I know you didn't," said Audrey.

Picking up the phone cradle with his left hand while holding the receiver to his ear with his right he rose from his chair and walked over to the window trailing the cable behind him. The snow had ceased falling. Down to his left he spotted Renshaw setting off on his beat and bitterly regretted his earlier needless moment of nostalgic spite. Every copper, he thought, sets out expecting the unexpected. Further on from the spire lay the new industrial estate on land that once housed the goods yard and to the left of that stood apartment blocks where the local gas works had once operated from. He remembered him and Pete walking past the up or down gasometers while heading for The Swiss Café and their games of chess. But ever present were the thirteen arches of the viaduct that he would climb up to with his train spotting books. He imagined a Castle Class thundering across making his day but could not imagine the dismantling of the gas works or the regeneration around goods yard. There was suddenly a longing for the warmth and the music of times long gone.

"You've left me again," said Audrey.

"Sorry," he said "just daydreaming."

"I never took you to be a day dreamer Samuel."

"Neither did I," he replied, "now what about his parents? You haven't mentioned them."

"They have split and he went to live with Susan. That is why she is so close to him. He is a good lad Samuel, just gone a little astray, he even told Susan himself about the cocaine, she had no idea. Now he just wants to stop but needs help."

He paused before telling her about young Baker and the confidence he had in him and how he would arrange for the two of them to meet.

"Now I don't want him arrested or taken into custody."

"That will not happen," he assured her.

"Why can't you go yourself?"

"Because he would not want an old fart like me calling on him."

"Now I would never call you an old fart Samuel."

"So, I have to ask what you would call me?"

"That is for me to know and for you never to find out," she replied.

"I will arrange that and tell him to go in plain clothes," he told her.

"Thank you, Samuel," she said.

"That's ok," he replied.

The snow started falling again and brought with it the faces of those who checked out the goods yard for German spies as the little engines shunted the freight cars around. He remembered walking into town for the first time on his own. So many firsts. The first smoke. The first kiss.

The first day at school. Every plane of experience seemed to flash before him in the way that life is supposed to before the end. Every phase chaptered in a library of whiteness covering all.

Benson knocked and walked in just as he was placing the phone back on his desk.

"Sorry Benson," he said, while looking at his watch. "I should have been with you in The Blue Room."

"No problem," said Benson.

"I've just been discussing Mannion," said Salt while gesturing towards the phone.

"So have we," Benson told him.

"Anything to report?"

"Quite a bit sir, in the strongroom there were two safes," said Benson, getting straight to the point, "and both were unlocked. We think that maybe he was checking stuff before taking his life."

"What kind of stuff?"

"Ledgers and receipts and invoices going way back and ninety thousand pounds in cash."

"Ninety thousand pounds!" exclaimed Salt.

"Yes sir."

"Any conclusions?"

"Money laundering for a start," said Benson, "we found letters from his bank questioning the amount of cash he paid in but he had the perfect answer by saying that many purchasers paid for their jewellery in cash."

"That ties in with what he told Turner." Said Salt.

"It does sir but there are other factors."

"Such as?"

"The regular cash payments that Campbell received came from Mannion."

"That can be proved?"

"More or less, yes."

"How do you mean, more or less?"

"We came across a personal notebook listing cash payments to various people."

"And Campbell was listed?"

"Well, no, but between them Crockett and Briggs worked out that payments made to a certain Elgar coincided with the dates Campbell paid those amounts into his bank."

"So, he used a pseudonym?"

"Yes."

"And there were others?"

"Yes sir, two others, not as much as Campbell received but still substantial."

"And their names?"

"Bach and Beethoven."

"And you have no idea about the identities of these two?"

"Not yet sir, but it is being worked on."

After Benson had left the room Salt sat back in his chair and swivelled it to once more look out at the falling flakes as every aspect of the case appeared to spin out on to a revolving stage with all the players taking their turns to come in to view.

The dreamers of the night rely on

peering past a darkened sky.

Chapter Fifteen

The Wheel of Fortune

He imagined Gerald pulling pints and keeping a clean cellar looking to the outside world like the perfect publican chatting away to the face on the other side of the bar with a demeanour suited to the personality of the recipient making him the perfect host. But Gerald was also dealing drugs. Salt found great difficulty in associating a drugs baron with the mate he walked to school with every day, sharing the not unusual distinction of wearing shoes with cardboard covering holes. If it had been Colly, he could have believed it.

Looking back, he realised that at that time they were still suffering the consequences of the second world war. But kids were kids and were oblivious to such repercussions even if they did need a coupon from the ration book for the special times when they were allowed a few sweets.

He recalled Niel Dalgliesh coming to their school. Some Scottish kid with a funny accent who, unlike him and most of his mates was dressed immaculately. He remembered fainting at morning assembly and being taken outside to sit on a step with his head between his legs and Mr Hollingsworth asking him if he had had breakfast. It also occurred to him that neither Stinky or Colly would think in the way that he was thinking now. But they had never been away to know what it was like to come back.

Campbell, he thought, was most probably an extremely efficient accountant who had built up a loyal trusting clientele before succumbing to the availability of easy money. Most likely the dirty side of the drugs business was pushed to the back of his mind or never even contemplated as such funds fell so easily into his pocket. The cash cushioned his conscience and immunised him against the immorality of destroying people's lives.

Looking out to sea from his castle on the coast bought with his ill-gotten gains cut him off from the reality and the upshot of his actions.

He would never have pulled a trigger but what he triggered was just as sinister.

Penny Campbell presented him with a dilemma. Every time he thought about her; he could not help but see that beautiful face looking into the mesmerised eyes of a ragged arsed council house kid. The encounter had never left him. That understanding smile was just as penetrative today as it was all those years ago. He did not want her to be guilty of condoning her husband's actions but he also knew that his stance was illogical. As it had been with Kathy.

He heard the geese before he saw them which brought him again to the window. He guessed they were overhead having taken off from the pool in the park. When they did come into view, he counted nine in their usual delta formation. He watched them winging over the bell tower of the town hall still cackling away heading south west which he knew would take them over One Way Wood and Clubbie's cottage and the Old Farm and probably onto one of the pools feeding Black Bag Mill, but suddenly they veered to the right.

Now they were heading towards the industrial conurbation starting just beyond the town. Soon they would be flying over the rolling mills and the foundries and factories that once employed thousands but now lay like empty mausoleums to the world of work. He remembered kneeling on the bed in his little bedroom wearing his blue striped pyjamas, looking out in awe at what appeared to a brilliant sunset, but he knew it was caused by the opening of the furnaces from the distant steel works which eventually shut its gates forever. Almost every leaver from every surrounding school found employment in such places.

But for him it was the building trade through Dickie Dartford who placed him with a superb craftsman by the name of William Smith. "Call me Billy," said the older man to his young protégé when they were first introduced. He recalled Billy sending him to the bottom of the site on his first day with a wheelbarrow to pick up a bag of cement only to find that such a weight was way beyond his scrawny frame. Passing by was the ganger of the navvies who was a gorilla of a man with no neck and orangutan type arms.

"Excuse me sir," he said to the gorilla, "would you help me to pick up this bag of cement please?"

"Pick it up your fucking self," came the harsh reply.

Walking past at the same time was another man who he later got to know as Kenn the carpenter.

Not only did Kenn give the gorilla a roasting but he also picked up the bag and placed it in the wheelbarrow.

"Thank you, sir," said Salt.

"That's ok," said Kenn, and with a smile added. "Any problems on this site come and see me"

"I will sir."

"Just one thing young man," said Kenn.

"Yes sir."

"Remember you are not at school now, not that kind anyway."

It was a lesson he never forgot and one which served him well during those early years on the beat and in his time doing National Service and his eventual move to London.

The geese finally disappeared out of sight and although he could no longer see them, he imagined them still winging to their destination. "There are moments when the soul takes wings," he remembered again, "and what it needs to go to, to that it flies."

The phone rang, it was Mary. "I've just seen something I thought might interest you," she said.

"Where are you?" he asked.

"At the hospice shop."

"Well?"

"Kathy came in," she said.

"What did she say?"

"She didn't."

"You didn't speak."

"No"

"Why not?"

"I wasn't sure at first if it was her," she told him. "After all, how many years has it been? Anyway, she sailed passed me standing at the till and went right to the back of the shop. Never even looked my way.""

"And?"

"And there waiting for her was the manager, they seemed to be having words."

"Arguing you mean."

"Yes."

"You didn't hear what was said?"

"They were whispering."

"So, how do you know they were arguing?"

"Well, she had her back to me but I could see that his face was like thunder. He turned away from her twice to stare up at the ceiling but turned back to put his face right up to hers, on the second occasion she tried to push him away but he grabbed her arm and then her handbag and reached in and pulled out a package."

"Then what?"

"They just stood staring at each other for what seemed an eternity before she grabbed her bag back then spun round to storm out of the shop."

"And that was it."

"Not quite," she said, "as she was walking out, she bumped into Edna, almost knocking her over."

"So, who is Edna?" asked Salt.

"The other assistant," she told him. "And she was none too pleased and went on to tell me that Kathy had been in several times just recently along with Lizzie White's brother."

"You are sure she said that?"

"Why would I say it if she had not?"

"Sorry," he said.

"So you should be," she told him, and then asked if he would be home for dinner.

"Yes," he said, "I will be home for dinner."

"And that's a promise?"

"That's a promise."

Some might have thought that they were in the home straight. But not Salt. He knew that there was one massive hurdle facing him and it was not Beechers Brook. It was proof. He also knew it was highly probable that within days they could close down the drug dealing and make arrests but that would not necessarily flush out the one who gave the nod to Ulrich. Turner could very well be right, he thought, about Robin's involvement, but questioned if he was the one hiring the hitman to carry out his proxy killings. He also doubted any of those involved viewed themselves as villains but just saw their dealing as serving a social need while lining their pockets at the same time.

He was desperately sorry to hear about Kathy's involvement but realised it was something he should have picked up on. The Jockey, after all, was another perfect front for legitimising their tainted profits, and her telling him about the cash supposedly found in the safe after Gerald's death should have rung alarm bells, especially with Mannion being such a regular visitor. He was convinced that under normal circumstances a man of Mannion's persuasion would not have touched The Jockey with the proverbial bargepole. Back in London the alarm bells would have been off the scale. His judgement would not have been impaired by his past inveigling the present. There was though, one thing he was sure of, and that was that Kathy believed her husband's death was an accident. But why was he murdered? Had he decided to call time on his drug dealing and had Campbell come to the same decision? Decisions that might have cost them and Penny Campbell their lives. After all they were not criminals, unlike the criminal who masterminded their demise. If it had not been for the vigilance of Albert Hackett looking through that letter box in Stepping Street and reporting what he saw none of this would have kicked off. Anyone else finding Penny Campbell might have thought she had died naturally in her sleep and the real reason might not have emerged. But kick off it did, just as he had returned for an easy life.

He now had extra balls to juggle. Briggs was even talking about the possible involvement of South American cartels, but was it simply the charity shop manager who was the baron behind this whole dirty business. In most crime novels it was nearly always the most unlikely who emerged. But this was not a crime novel. This was real. Many were suffering because of the felonious actions of a few.

He arranged a meeting in The Blue Room for early the next morning. Even Bychkov was coming up from North Devon. They would hammer out every detail gathered so far. Allow any suspicions to be aired whether fanciful or not. Even if it took all day, he wanted each one of them to add as many coals to the fire as possible. Measuring twice and cutting once was an adage that had served him well down the years. He wanted a water tight case to put before the C.P.S. A case that he knew would not entail a dramatic Hollywood ending.

There would be no sudden revelation in the heat of the night or a shoot-out at Culbone with bullets bouncing off the ancient gravestones and the iron cross. No motor boat chase across Combe Bay or a hairy confrontation on the dangerous narrow path leading down to The Valley of the Rocks as the feral goats looked on from their perilous jagged-edged perches. He doubted he would spot a crop duster flying low over Clubbie's cottage before it tried to hunt him down as he sought refuge in his grandad's fields of wheat. Or gather everyone together in some spooky country house before finally revealing the guilty party. But with a smile he did imagine a car chase through the winding lanes leading to Hill Church where they manged to box the villain in at the entrance to Black Bag Mill. Only for him to jump out of his car and sprint away with young Baker in pursuit. After vaulting the safety fence, the villain made his way up the slope above the wheel but slipped and fell into one of the buckets which took him down into the water without him coming back up.

A fantasy ending he knew would please both his mother and his grandmother who were big Edgar Wallace fans. Perhaps, he thought, it would become a cold case in twenty or thirty years when he was no longer of this planet. Maybe they would bring Turner and Bychkov back to head a new investigation. It was still possible of course that he would end it here and now but fresh doubts brought the feeling that this was not the way this story was meant to end and his bloody mindedness not to let a failure determine his career did not somehow seem so desperately important. He pulled his touchstone from his pocket and rolled it around in the palm of his hand while looking out at the arctic whiteness still covering the town. Still covering the cracks that he knew would still be there after the thaw.

Maybe it was to melt away he thought.

Maybe Mary was right and it was time to go bathing off Bondi Beach or make the climb up to Machu Pichu or fly off to his Californian friend to enable them to make the pilgrimage to Salinas.

Suddenly there was an endless number of maybes with so little time to fit them all in. Maybe he would even start putting pen to paper.

In the Blue Room they were getting fidgety. It was not normal for Salt to be late. Benson checked his watch and being aware of his boss's antipathy towards tardiness of any kind left his desk to go and check on him. Turner left hers to go to the window to look up to the three sycamores on the distant ridge. The phone rang on Bensons desk and no one seemed to want to answer so she turned and picked up the receiver.

"Is it possible to speak to Sergeant Benson?" said a female voice.

"I'm afraid he has just left the office," said Turner.

"Will he be away long?" asked the voice.

"Only a few minutes I suspect," Turner told her.

"Then I'll ring back later," said the voice.

"Give me your name and number and I will get him to ring you when he returns," said Turner.

"Just tell him it's Rita," came the reply.

"Rita?" asked the young detective.

"Yes, just tell him its Rita from The Belvedere."

So spins the wheel of life and love
of all below
and all above
through every day and every night
bringing us darkness
and the light.

The End.

9 781835 386804